James McIntyre
The Mammoth Cheese

a novel

by

John Passfield

Rock's Mills Press
Oakville, Ontario
2022

The poems in this novel which were written by the historical James McIntyre (1827–1906) are identified in the journal, *The Making of James McIntyre: The Mammoth Cheese*, which is available for free access on the author's website. The complete McIntyre poems are available at other sites on the internet.

Published by
Rock's Mills Press

Cover Design: Craig Passfield
Cover Illustration: A photograph of the Ingersoll Mammoth Cheese of 1866.
Author's Website: www.johnpassfield.ca
Publisher's Website: www.rocksmillspress.com

Chapter 1
Ingersoll 1

Not sifting through the ruins of the great ten-year contretemps at Troy. Not shifting blackened beams from off the well in search of a cold bucket of water to drink on a hot, humid day.

The monster's wiles I will defeat.

Standing on the porch, in the early morning, of my house, here in my home town of Ingersoll.

It is peaceful

A man standing on a porch.
A poet who writes occasional verse.
A visitor who is being interviewed.

as I sit here

Why do you want to write an epic?
Are your lyric poems not enough?
Your everyday poems about Ingersoll?

by the river.

Peasants driven off the land.
Swimming in a lake.
The laying of a cornerstone.

Not standing outside the theatre on the banks of the Thames. Not checking the ropes that secure the horses so they don't shy at the trumpet blast to announce the new play.

Life, like a dome of many coloured glass.

Taking a deep breath of the fresh morning air as the sun comes up over the trees. Saying, to myself, what I say every morning. Who wouldn't want to live here? – in Ingersoll?

A boy was born in London.

We have seen thee Queen of Cheese
Laying quietly at your ease
Gently fanned by evening breeze –
Thy fair form no flies dare seize.

"Too bad about his first wife."
"The carriage bolted after church."

A bucket
of rich foamy cream.

An effusion of opulent bliss - roles diverge - make a fresh start - not worth
the candle - you might well ask - a soul-searing thought-experience - many an
expert - shifting blackened beams - such ill-omens - an underground grape-
vine.

Do I feel welcome in your fair city? Thank you for giving me the keys.
Thank you for opening the gates and portals and doors.

Two answers contended
to be the answer
to a question.

Not slogging through ankle-deep mud in the swamps at Missolongli. Not
slipping into the tent to check the mosquito-netting that keeps the creatures
from attacking Milord's face.
Place now you look for it in vain.
Walking along the path that leads to the town. Life in the country – life in
the town. The best of both.

A boy was born in Broadbridge Heath.

All gaily dressed soon you'll go
To the great Provincial Show
To be admired by many a beau
in the city of Toronto.

Early morning in Ingersoll.
Walking through the town.

A bucket
of fresh cool milk.

In the midst of battle - deeper than the deepest rift - where do I put myself -
a strange question - have you thought - some other prize - the rest of it - stand-
ing on a porch - among the debris - the judges' decisions.

Have I been in your fair city before? I feel as if I am seeing everything with
the original opening of my eyes. I feel as if I have lived here all my life.

Two rivers
flowed
to the sea.

Not clinging to the mast in the Bay of Lerici as the waves crash into the
bow. Not reefing the sails and pointing the prow against the howling wind.
Thoughts that do often lie too deep for tears.
Walking over the recent bridge that spans the creek. Calling hello to some
early risers. Much more sturdy than the one that washed away.

A hero setting forth on a great adventure.
A community undertaking a major enterprise.
A chronicler of the history of his time.

Cows numerous as swarm of bees –
Or as leaves upon the trees –
It did require to make thee please
And stand unrivalled Queen of Cheese.

The railway crosses the continent as my love crosses your heart.

Homer was fond of ancient cheese.
Oft mentioned in his Odyssey.

Do you know what an epic is?
Any idea how many books?
Any idea how many words?

Humans and angels are different.

With Shakespeare one should never compare oneself.
Shakespeare alone is perched on the topmost shelf.

There was a boy who was born in Forres, Scotland, and emigrated to Upper

Canada and settled in Ingersoll.

Once there were two suns in the human sky. Six months summer from one. Six months summer from the other. One burnt out. The other continued to shine.

Opening a new railway line.
Hunting mink and fox and coon.
Watching wild deer roaming free.

Oh Mr. Harris he doesn't sit in a Dumferling hall.
He sits in his office in Ingersoll.

Not tip-toeing as I enter the room above the Spanish Steps in Rome. Not trying to avoid disturbing the young poet as he lies asleep.
Worthy of either song or story.
Walking along the main street. Everything here that a family could want. Not a service that this town cannot provide. The feel of a solid sidewalk under one's feet.

A boy was born in Moorgate.

May you not receive a scar as
We have heard that Mr. Harris
Intends to send you off as far as
The great World's show at Paris.

"Tell him your grandma's having a birthday – he'll write a poem."
"Show up at the house and read to her what he wrote."

A bucket
of clear spring water.

A major diversion - the step is firm - the fastest bullet - sits and figures - it all started - a certificate of significance - the windows of my house - to nourish me - shy at the trumpet blast - present the logic.

What is my purpose while I am here in your fair city? My purpose is to experience all of life – or at least as much of it as I can. My purpose is to respond to that life-experience in the form of art.

One path
was a circle.

Not holding the jar of arsenic as I contemplate my poems. Not thinking of this dingy attic as my last glimpse of life here on this ungrateful earth.

O what can ail thee knight at arms.

Bigger and better than my former establishment. Applying my key to the sturdy door. The better to serve you madame or sir. These premises are higher and dryer – safer too.

A boy was born in Bristol.

Of the youth – beware of these –
For some of them might rudely squeeze
And bite your cheek; then songs or glees
We could not sing o' Queen of Cheese.

Arriving at the furniture emporium.
Another day at the store.

A bucket
with nothing inside.

A book with great ideas - should something occur - making honey for the hive - a story of dreadful news - thoughts that chase each other - a tour of myself - expect an adherence - some vow to stay - giving me the keys - little angel-images.

You desire to interview me? But I was planning to interview you. You are, by far, the much more interesting of the two.

Two horses
pull
the cart.

Opening the front door of the establishment of yours truly – James Mc-Intyre, prominent citizen of Ingersoll, in the province of Ontario, in the country of Canada. Furniture-maker, cabinetmaker, and reluctant undertaker. Also newspaper reporter and occasional poet – when occasion serves.

For there the bloodhound dare not chase.

I catch the butterfly as it wings. I catch the sunlight on the trees. Record the sparkles on the stream as they pass us by. I catch the bubbles – one could say – before they burst.

We'rt thou suspended from balloon
You'd cast a shade, even at noon;
Folks would think it was the moon

About to fall and crush them soon.

If the sky should send down pearls, in the form of raindrops, I would make a necklace for you.

An English youth to Canada came,

An open door on a busy street.
The daily, weekly, seasonal routines.
The sun in winter, summer, spring and fall.

A labourer, John Roe by name,

How long would an epic take to write?
Do you have time for such an undertaking?
Do you think you could do it in your spare time?

His little wealth had made him bold,
Twenty sovereigns in gold;

Tomorrow, though, all of life will become spectacular. It will be the grand unveiling of the seven-thousand pound Mammoth Cheese. The largest cheese to be manufactured in the British Empire. A feat whose renown will travel like lightning around the globe.
O no! it is an ever fixed mark.
First the gathering in the yard. Then the opening of the doors. The spectacular unveiling. Mouths will open up in awe. Then a few words from Mr. Harris, and of course the Mayor, and then I'll read my poem.

Chapter 2
Ingersoll 2

Bright and early down at Mr. Harris's factory. Didn't bother to open the furniture-shop. All the employees want to be here to see the unveil. The crowd waits outside the doors. Everyone prompt at nine o'clock. Plenty of rumours have gone around town. Many are here to have a look. Interesting to think that this cheese began as just an idea.

There are such things as fountains in the world.

I have my pencil and my notebook ready. Make a few jottings as things happen and then work out my article when I go back to the store. Mr. Hall will be waiting for my copy. Promised I'd have it by afternoon. I always take it over as soon as it's done. I always slide it onto the counter as I ask Mr. Hall if this is the office of the *New York Times*.

There is always

The placing of information on a grid.
A black void with fangs.
A door that is barred and then closed.

traffic

Where, exactly, were you born in Scotland?
In the country or in the town?
Just how Scottish do you consider yourself to be?

rumbling over the bridge.

Enjoying the sunbeam shining on the water.
Laying drain tiles to control the floods.
Visiting the lime-stone quarries.

I often think that there are thoughts that are deeper than our thoughts. Thoughts that are deeper than our dreams and nightmares tend to be. We awake in the midst of a dream or a nightmare and get a glimpse of our deeper thoughts. But we never awake to the deepest level of thought. There are diamonds at the deepest level of the mind.

When the green leaves were a-falling.

Sometimes I get the feeling that all of this is merely a dream. A dream with all the negatives filtered out.

What was the great work that he was born to write? What was the great undertaking that all his faculties throbbed to create? He would dedicate himself to that great endeavour. He would become the great poet that he felt he was born to be. Every tick of his watch was a burr that would spur him on.

"Sang for years in the choir."
"Then he quit."

I am a king outside the battlements! I am sitting on the grass! I have failed to take the castle!

My head is whirling round! What do I do now?

Everything rhymed - integral to the concern - roles collide - you will be human - a very probing question - look at me closely - start with something simple - seeing everything - a loaf of mouldering bread - what was the purpose.

So what is the epic adventure? The magic adventure that will lift a whole village and float it on the foams of far-flung seas? The adventure that will put Ingersoll in the realm of legend and myth?

Well it is a quest – a voyage – a searching. A village on the move. Seeking its destiny – seeking its essence – seeking its soul.

Rivalling the stories of ancient sagas. As bold as Balboa – or was it Cortez? The epic adventure will be the story of the Mammoth Cheese.

It was a question
that had so far
not been asked.

The doors open. The crowd surges. The wagon comes rolling out. A dozen men, at least, or twenty, wheeling the cart out into the yard. Mr. Harris waves his arms and the crowd moves back in respect. The cart stops and the crowd moves in again.

My barn is to build and my baby unborn.

When does cloud turn into sunshine? When does rumour turn into fact? How often in life does such a momentous event occur? Here is the flower of

Ingersoll agriculture. All these years of perfecting the cheese. All the cows who have chewed the cud out in the fields. A memory for everyone in attendance for many years.

What was the great work that he was born to write? What was the great undertaking that all his faculties throbbed to create? He would dedicate himself to that great endeavour. He would become the great poet that he felt he was born to be. Every tick of his watch was a burr that would spur him on.

Morning at the cheese factory.
The unveiling of the Mammoth Cheese.

I am a king inside the battlements! I am sitting on the wall! I have failed to defend the castle! My head is whirling round! What do I do now?

Sense a crime - often fall short - brush off the snow - is that a good sign - chief aim - what is the definition - the waves crash - stealing a moment - it can find you - such heights of perfection.

The cheese will be exhibited here – close to home – in North America. It will astound the people who behold it with its massive size. It is a seven-thousand pound block of succulent cheese.
Made in factories in tiny Ingersoll. The product of eight hundred contributing cows. The wonder of modern agricultural feats.
It will win all available prizes. Sweep the judges off their feet. Garner publicity that will reach across the waves.

Actually,
one was less than a river –
it was a trickle of a creek.

A group of monks went out walking. Each monk was absorbed in the depths of thought. Each was thinking of higher concerns. Each was seeking the centre of his own being. Each monk was alone in the universe.
We receive but what we give.
We'll go for a walk after church. It's so pleasant with the leaves on the forest floor. Hum the hymns that raised the rafters an hour before.

Lightning traveling around the globe.
An article about a major event.
A somber train ride home.

These thoughts stick in my mind as a wagon leaves tracks in the mud.

Made from goats, preferred to cows,
Which on the mountainside would browse.

Ever think about your mother?
Many thoughts about your dad?
A sad day, was it, when you said goodbye to them?

Angels and humans are not the same.

However, were Shakespeare to come back today to life,
Whether he rests in peace or in strife,

He always thought that he had a talent to write.

Paths lead upward. Paths lead downward. There is a golden mean on every path.

Buying railway bonds.
A poem composed during a banquet.
A town with a new water-works.

Oh Mr. Harris, he came to the town of Ingersoll.
Now his factory is the biggest one of them all.

The crowd is silent. The crowd is in awe. The crowd surges around the cart. Seven thousand pounds of beautiful Ingersoll cheese. The ingenuity of the Ingersoll factories. The product of eight hundred Ingersoll cows. The product of planning and execution. An emblem of all that is good in this town. The product of thousands of years of perfecting the making of cheese.
For God's sake hold your tongue and let me love.
To hear of the great endeavour as you go about your rounds. To read of it in the newspaper as a coming event. To hear of some exquisite art-work on the other side of the earth – a Mona Lisa, a David, the ceiling of a chapel – and then to see a great human achievement in one's home town. There is no comparison I can think of at a time like this. I promised to capture this for the newspaper. I should merely print a blank page when I print my report.

What was the great work that he was born to write? What was the great undertaking that all his faculties throbbed to create? He would dedicate himself to that great endeavour. He would become the great poet that he felt he was born to be. Every tick of his watch was a burr that would spur him on.

"He designed and built the first house for his first wife."
'Then for his second wife he went and did it again."

I need a dozen catapults to take the battlements! I need a dozen cauldrons of pitch to defend the walls! With this weapon I could defeat the combatants in record time! I sit on the grass and on the battlements! My head is throbbing as if it is about to split in two!

Alive and buzzing - raps sharply on the door - to write a story - what does it mean - on that basis - humans and angels - somehow unconnected - a book in itself - the top of the staircase - everything else flows.

To England, next, across the ocean. To be exhibited and admired. A great popular wave which will inundate British shores.

England – the centre of the world. The arbiter of thought of the whole Empire. This phenomenon will be presented – at court – to the Queen.

How can she fail to respond to its flavour? To respond to its massive, imperial size? Surely knighthood will be conferred on this block of cheese.

One path
was a line.

A group of monks went out walking. They knew not where they walked. Each monk was absorbed in the depths of thought. As they walked they trampled the monastery garden. The garden in which they had toiled the day before.

Moving about in worlds not realized.

The leisure-furniture by the door. Rocking chairs and such. The kitchen tables off to the side. The beds and baby-cradles further back.

What was the great work that he was born to write? What was the great undertaking that all his faculties throbbed to create? He would dedicate himself to that great endeavour. He would become the great poet that he felt he was born to be. Every tick of his watch was a burr that would spur him on.

Mr. Harris the Ingersoll hero.
Requesting an interview.

Whan that Aprille with his shoures soote,
The droghte of March hath perced to the roote,
And bathed every veyne in swich licóur
Of which vertú engendred is the flour;
Whan Zephirus eek with his swete breeth
Inspired hath in every holt and heeth
The tendre croppes, and the yonge sonne
Hath in the Ram his halfe cours y-ronne,
And smale foweles maken melodye,

That slepen al the nyght with open ye,
So priketh hem Natúre in hir corages,
Thanne longen folk to goon on pilgrimages.

If all I had - cast ourselves on the waters - the daily routine - opening of
my eyes - what is called 'imagery' - the human sky - not for everyone - too bad
it was swept away - the words on gravestones - tell a frightening tale - been
neglecting things.

Oh for sure this experience will happen. It will certainly happen for sure. For sure and for certain it will come to pass in time.

Every house needs a solid foundation. Every journey needs a plan and a route. Every quest needs a wily leader and intrepid adventurers to climb the mast and reef the sails.

The deed is as well as done. This is a story without suspense – it can be entered in the books. The Golden Fleece comes at the end of the old, old story, you see, but our story already has the Mammoth Cheese.

The cart
goes
East or West.

Speeches – speeches – speeches. Mr. Harris speaks first – points and says 'The Mammoth Cheese' and then stands down. The Mayor will be last, as I understand, but many, many Ingersollian rhetoricians seem to have interposed themselves in between. Everybody in town wants to rhapsodize on this topic on this marvelous day. I stop jotting down the names when the number reaches five. And to summarize what each is saying would take a whole tome. Still – their hearts are filled with gravy – their minds are filled with fine wine. It is a banquet that they are serving – a banquet of words.

The thrilling secrets of the birth of time.

To put into words what one truly feels. What one thinks and what one feels – both combined. That is the mode of communication that I strive for. Every poem is a new beginning – a chance to summarize what my heart is saying to me. What the Mayor is saying is fine – a noble sentiment on a noble occasion – but I don't think a speech in prose can compete with verse.

If the sea should wash up driftwood from the decks of ships, I would make a shelter for you.

He was industrious and wise

A block of cheese with no tragic flaw.
A special event in a stable-yard.

A bucket on a table in the rain.

And e'en small sums did not despise,

What was life like, for you, in Scotland?
Why did you decide to leave?
Why Canada, of all the places on the globe?

He added to his wealth each year
For independence he loved dear,

A group of monks went toiling. They toiled in the monastery garden. Surprised and saddened they were to see the devastation. As they toiled each monk was absorbed in his thoughts. Tomorrow they would go out for a walk.
The king sits in Dumferling town drinking the blood-red wine.
I join the Mayor up on the wagon. Mr. Harris has gone inside. On the other wagon lies the Mammoth Cheese. A proud day for Ingersoll. A proud day for the British Empire. I thank the Mayor – my fellow citizens – I clear my throat. A slight breeze, but I manage to hold the paper steady. Don't want to stumble over my precious words. All my friends and neighbours are here to hear me read.

We have seen thee Queen of Cheese
Laying quietly at your ease
Gently fanned by evening breeze
Thy fair form no flies dare seize …

Chapter 3
Ingersoll 1

The Mammoth Cheese sits on a cart outside Mr. Harris's factory. Flexing its trophy-winning muscles in the glorious sun. Though I have to admit that it's not so glorious when encased in its travel-box. But the box is sturdy and well-constructed – a wise precaution, I am no doubt sure. The cheese will spread its wings – in all its glory – when we reach the scene of our triumph – Saratoga, New York.

Far below our world's centre.

The furniture-store will take care of itself – yes, the store will take care of itself. The workers will stand on the sidewalk and watch us walk by. But this is my day away from the store. This, for me, is an 'Immersed-in-a-Mammoth Cheese' kind of day. Travelling to Saratoga, New York. Writing of the trip and the town and the people. Writing of the gleaming of the trophy as the massive cheese emerges from behind the clouds of obscurity and throws its arms around its prodigal brother, the reluctant sun.

I come and sit

A uniform with medals on the chest.
Two poets chasing each other around Europe.
A faulty belt on a lathe.

by the river

Are you aware of the size and shape of an epic poem?
How many books do you think there are in the *Iliad*?
Do you think you'll be able to write that many books?

as often as I can.

An old fellow with a young bride.
A toast to universal brotherhood.

A park named after the Queen.

Scotland is my ancestral homeland. Born on a farm near Forres, I was. Like everyone, I had a mom and a dad. Well, not like everyone perhaps. A dad might be dead before a child is born. Or – God forbid – a mother might perish in childbirth. But no such ill-omens attended – beclouded – be-shrouded my own unheralded birth.

Unless we make this correction.

Writing is an extension of the mind. Writing is an extension of the arm. The mind and the arm meet on the page. Where those two meet – that is the poem. The poem is what one thinks and how one feels.

The family of a poet. Mad-men, sailors, ladies and lords. Marriage for money – a ruined estate. Brutal tempers – tumultuous remorse. A death from tuberculosis and a broken heart.

"He loves this town."
"He really does."

My old friend and I sifting through the burnt-out ruins of Troy. Slaking our thirst with a charred wooden bucket. A welcome draught of cold water from a well. "I don't know, James," Homer mutters as I help him pick his way among the debris. "Before we came here, it seemed like such a good idea. But who would want to read an epic on the fall of Troy?"

Can you manage - turn their stories into rhyme - discussion of odds - a tiny technical glitch - reveals the thought - rift on the ocean floor - experience all of life - through thick and thin - two aspects of a theme - the world i inhabit.

Did I enjoy the tour of the town? All the significant local sights? Where to get one's shoes polished and where to dine?

They say that rooted people make the best sailors. They say that this is because they have a clear sense of home. It is as if they have swallowed a compass as they sail the seven seas.

I have roots in the hills of Scotland – I have roots in Ingersoll. I put down roots in every place where I hang my hat. Roots are what connects the mind to the soil.

What if the question
does not suit you?,
asked Answer One of Answer Two.

The photographer sets up his camera. He paces off the distance to the Mammoth Cheese. A ladder is put in place and people climb up and take their places on top of the Mammoth Travel-box. Many children, I see, as is appropriate, I'm thinking, for the occasion. The great men of this great achievement arrange themselves around the wagon. Mr. Harris to the right in modest pose. I scribble a few quick notes in planting the seeds of tomorrow's news. The camera-powder flashes and history is immobilized.

Each one doth know it is not wise.

The recording of significant events. Words have sufficed for so many years – and have never lost their appeal, that is for sure. Will never lose their appeal, if I have anything to say. But the invention of photography – what a wonder of the age! To capture life! – as it is! – on the very day! One can only regret – when in a thoughtful mood – that we do not have – cannot have – a photograph of Shakespeare taking his bow at the end of the play. William Shakespeare! – in his habit! – as he lived!

Born a duke, or an earl, or at least a baronet. Disagreed with England's ancient social divide.

Handed out pamphlets on street corners. 'God is an atheist – so am I!' Wrote poems of exquisite beauty to birds and the wind.

The unveiling of the protective cheese-box.
A photographic record of the event.

My friend is feeling downcast. "Right now, James," he mutters, "it's all bits and pieces in my mind." We are sitting by the fire. We have spent most of the day shoring up the sagging sheep-fold with brambles and thorns. "It's a huge undertaking and my eyes are going bad and I might go blind." The iron-age pot is coming to the boil.

Inclusion in the discussion - standing outside of yourself - one set of footprints - devoid of blood - purpose is to respond - your innermost longings - a gradual awakening - what you've accomplished - no one wishes to share - secrets that are kept.

I feel as if I could thrive here. I feel as if I am thriving now. Every atom in the air is food for the mind.

I love to stand on the sidewalk outside my store. People I know – people I don't know – people of youth – people of age. Everyone going about the business of their lives.

I often think of a town as a beehive. People buzzing from here to there. Gathering nectar from the flowers they meet on the way.

And the other
was more than a river –
it was a torrent in full force.

The factories processed the milk. Separated the curds and the whey. They employed eight-hundred cows. The Ranneys broached the idea to Mr. Harris. Mr. Harris is the leader. In his factory is where the gigantic cheese-wheel was made. The Ranneys and Mr. Galloway are partners as well.

This is the source of all my grief.

Sitting on the bench beside the river. Trying to capture what I am thinking in incandescent words:

My friends, we sing Canadian themes,
For in them we proudly glory;
Her lakes, her rivers and her streams,
Worthy of renown in story.

A little boy who used to laugh and sing.
Two writers holding horses outside a theatre.
A penny dropped into a well.

These memories come back to nourish me as a bucket of water from a neglected well.

We can see, on ancient vases,
Shepherds taking mid-day pauses,

Are you aware of the many rules concerning epics?
Are you willing to adhere to every one of these rules?
Do you realize that readers expect an adherence to epic form?

Humans think in imagery.

He would, no doubt, be very, very pleased
To bend his talents to the praise of cheese.

When still a boy he would turn his thoughts into rhymes.

There is a time for everything beneath the sun. When the clock claps its hands, it will be your time.

A hammer being tossed at the games.
A city well-served by railway lines.
Firemen racing to a fire.

Puzzling out the structure of my epic poem.
If a block of cheese sets out on a voyage, there must be something that it is

seeking. Then it follows that it cannot be seeking, of course, itself – the block of cheese.

The Mammoth Cheese, on its cart, slowly making its way to the train station. The prize oxen keep a steady pull on the load. The streets are lined with well-wishers as it rumbles over the newly-constructed bridge and down the main street in front of all the stores. A Roman triumph in the thoroughfares of Pompeii. I break away from the cheering throng and fling open the door and slap my notes on the counter of the *New York Times*. The latest tide in the affairs of the populace, Mr. Hall! I re-join the adoring multitude. Beaming! – beaming with pride! Back in time to see the Mammoth Cheese gracing the pavement outside the front door of my new establishment.

But this one fact we won't deny.

A departure, for sure, from my usual mode of practice. Mr. Hall and I have an iron-clad agreement – that Mr. Hall will never change a single word. Does 'meal' mean the same as 'repast'?, I asked him, when the question first arose. It's a matter of 'nuance', a matter of 'tone', a matter of 'style'. My name on the tail of an article has to mean something to me or it can never mean a thing to those who read. I would rather face oblivion – write no articles at all – than to have another writer speak for me. But today is different – today is a departure – today I lower my standards a tiny iota. I pick up my glove and I withdraw – the seconds sheath the pointed rapiers. How could I write and still have time to catch the train?

Born in a stable. Humble it was. Father died of a fractured skull. Left a legacy that he was never to collect. Lived in poverty all his life as poets have done.

"His second wife gave him stability when he needed it."
"No doubt she came along at just the right time."

How to reassure my friend? He is old and going blind and has never tried to write an epic before. He strums a simple note or two on his lyre. "Well, I like what you have told me", I say, to reassure my friend. "Just start with something simple, like Agammenon's dream, and go on from there."

History repeating itself - such a simple plan - what is the meaning - asked the same question - speculative speculation - nothing inside - to see the logic - i am told - other angels know - the candles flickered.

Or I think of people as water – swelling a storm or a surging tide. Dripping from a down-spout into a rain-barrel. Giving sustenance to a traveller half-buried in the sand.

People – people – people. People bury you under their cares. People dig you out of the rubble of your despair.

People walk by and never notice you. People walk by and give you a smile. Every person on this earth is a life-line, offered or denied.

The line
touched the circle.

Doctor Johnson said that a second marriage is a triumph of hope over experience. In my case, it was a case of hope over despair. But it doesn't bear much thinking about. It's all smouldering inside the head – don't give it air.

And that substantial one of stone.

Stealing a moment from the business of the shop to write a poem. A poem on the charms of Ingersoll:

The Thames and tributary rills
Here they do drive numerous mills,
Enabling millers to compete,
To pay high price for oats and wheat.

Born of a father who died before fatherhood. Before the boy could establish his birth. Born of a mother who took in sewing and needlework. Born of people who could barely read and write. However, he had an uncle who was sexton of a church.

The Mammoth Cheese on the move.
A street of endless cheers.

Poetry to us is given
As stars beautify the heaven,
Or as sunbeams when they gleam,
Sparkling so bright upon the stream;
And the poetry of motion
Is ship sailing o'er the ocean.
Or, when the bird doth graceful fly,
Seeming to float upon the sky;
For poetry is the pure cream
And essence of the common theme.

Do you remember - clinging to the mast - the candles flickered - pleased to know - make a few jottings - a stale-mate - catch the bubbles - puzzling out the structure - things will be different - never distracted from duty - plenty of thoughts.

So who are the people in my life that I have treasured? Who are the people in my life who have given me grief? Who the people who are my honey? – who are my wine?

Who the boulders in my seed-field – waiting to snag and break the plough? The fly – the mosquito – the gnat? And most important of all, how do I decide?

I keep a book, in my mind, with every name written down. Beside each name I have made a prominent mark. Perhaps you are wondering what mark I will put beside your name.

The cart
goes
North or South.

The train station is a swarm of Ingersollians, half of whom say that they are going on the trek.

Half of those with luggage say that they have never been to the States – half of them say that they go there all the time. All are breathless as the Mammoth Cheese is hoisted – very carefully – onto the railway car. A cheer rises from harmonious throats in the morning air. Plenty of room inside the railway car – plenty of room to include a trophy from Saratoga, New York.

He entered through an ancient mine.

The train has been a marvelous invention. If it wasn't for the oceans, one could write that the trains have created an unbroken girdle around the entire globe. Now come, come, come, come, come – another phrase for 'a broken girdle'. What could I write instead of those words? If I leave it, it will come to me – neither to sugar nor to honey will words sometimes yield. I shall have plenty of time to think as I sit on the train. I'm sure I'll be able to think of something else.

If the wind should blow seeds from exotic locations, I would create a magnificent garden for you.

He knew a laborer he would be

The milk from eight-hundred cows.
A bird who builds a nest.
A last-minute rumour sweeping a crowd.

Forever in the old country,

Have you considered that there are twenty-four books in an epic?
And that every book in an epic is a book in itself?
And each of these books is filled with dramatic episodes?

His forefathers had tilled the ground

And never one had saved a pound.

The engine chugs along the countryside. Farms and houses on display. The aisles are packed with Ingersollians. Moving in surges up and down. Who is on board and who is not is hard to tell. The whole town seemed to want to come along. Keats's narrator wondered where everyone had gone. Well they went to celebrate the big occasion, of course, though they didn't know that none would ever return. Well – on to Saratoga. With us it's a couple of spectacular days and we'll be back home.

You'll find they are but idle dreams.

"The poetry of James McIntyre is not for everyone. In fact, if one could say that the quality of his verse is in reverse proportion to the number of his readers, then we could rank his poetry as very high on the scale of quality indeed. Alone in the crow's nest of his talent, he peers at fertile lands that only he, among his readers, is able to see."

Chapter 4
Saratoga 1

Saratoga. The train station. Saratoga, New York. Had a look at Niagara Falls as we crossed on the bridge. Quite a crowd pouring off the train. Find the baggage car for my bags. Got some poems in there that I wouldn't want to lose. Watch the crew bring the wagon to the car where the mammoth monster has been stored. Pleased to hear that there was no damage to the cheese.

Then felt I like some watcher of the skies.

One crowd flows into another, as one stream flows into another stream. All the people from Ingersoll – so many I can hardly believe. People from other places who took the train to this place. All flowing out onto the street and joining the crowd who have spent their lives in this very town. Of course the train does not leave empty. People wave tickets and climb aboard. The conductor blows his whistle. One tide flows out and another tide flows in.

I sit on the bench

A man who refuses to be interviewed.
A certificate which is passed from hand to hand.
A person checking the shelves.

and take out my pencil

How did you find yourself in Ingersoll?
What made you come and settle here?
Did you hear about it in Scotland or after you came?

and my paper.

A programme for a music concert.
The stone walls of a sturdy farmhouse.
A bounteous crop of grain.

How deep does the mind go? I've often wondered. Deeper than plummet can possibly sound? Deeper than the deepest mine, whether of briny salt or sparkling gold? Deeper than the deepest rift at the nadir of the ocean floor?

One of your family I must have now.

Make the best of this, I say to myself. Make the best of this opportunity to shine.

Descended of kings and suicides. Borrowed money – massive debts. Flights from creditors on hobbled legs. A father dead – an uncle insane. A childhood thoroughly soaked in poetical lore.

"He's a better furniture-maker than a poet."
"That's for sure."

There is a staircase in front of me! Each stair is made of cloud! I walk towards the staircase! I put my foot on a stair! The step is firm!

Thorns in the pathway - my idea at first - letting blood - only move forward - gather the information - the clock would change - ashes of the phoenix - such a good idea - stronger and stronger wind - place them on a grid.

So what, for me, would be a typical writing day? Well, some days are typical, some are not. Some days are special – we have a sale at the store or a delivery wagon gets stuck in the mud – but many days are predictable routine.

How do I live and how do I write? How do I write and how do I live? To me, they go together – they're both the same.

I live to write and I also write to live.

What if the question
does not suit you?,
asked Answer Two of Answer One.

Meeting the local reporter. Breakfast in a charming little café. Comparison and contrast. His fair city – my fair city. Larger size – smaller size. Local attractions – spectacular scenes. What it's like to pound the beat and churn out the words. Special access for the press at every event.

No sound is dissonant which tells of life.

Half of my mind is on vacation – half of my mind is certainly not. I am here as an Ingersoll tourist, taking in the sights and walking around – but the other half of me is a reporter for the Ingersoll press. Every penny that people spend is to have a good read. This young reporter is very charming, but I sense a flaw in his eyes. He is a little too off-guard should something occur. I glance around as he chatters idly. I am a little more alert than my friend seems to be.

Married a girl but didn't love her. Fell in love with her circumstance. Fell in love with someone else. Now she was worse than when she was rescued by the poet. Drowned herself in the Serpentine.

Arriving in Saratoga.
A trainload of Ingersollians.

Each step is a risky move! Each step is made of cloud! What if my foot were to fall right through? I place each foot upon the stair! Each step takes me closer to the sun!

A massive dream - there are diamonds - cannot be seeking itself - now is not the time - your innermost soul - roots are what connects - information on a grid - to carry the standard - a gigantic book - put the blinders on.

Every experience comes to me as a package encased in rhyme. Take the word, 'incandescent'. What would rhyme, you might wonder, with this word?

Now it isn't a case of chasing after a rhyme. The rhyme must be integral to the concern. Art must have a central purpose – a central idea.

Each work of art – even an epic of great length – how many words are in *The Iliad*? – how many words tell the story of the founding of Rome? – must always be about one simple thing. Twenty-four books – a central idea – a central concern.

But the sea was
definitely a sea.

A fishing boat plied the waters of the ocean. The fishermen cast their nets into the sea. Today, perhaps, the catch would be what they hoped for. It had been, for them, a disappointing voyage. The catch was sparse and meager to this day.

The mind-forged manacles I hear.

It was a thrill the day we put up the sign. Had to borrow the big ladder from the stable. The sign still says '*McIntrye and Son*'.

A day of races at the track.
The office of the New York Times.
An adventure that starts as an everyday event.

Those times we spent together are as bricks mortared into a wall.

Eating snacks of bread and cheese,
A bite of which a god would please.

You have an affinity with people?
Love to stand outside your shop?
Love to chat with people about the town's affairs?

Humans think in prose.

We would have The Tragedy of Omelette,
A play that you would not forget.

Every subject was stained by the ink of his pen.

The river will empty into the sea. The sea will empty into the ocean. Every drop in the ocean will evaporate into the sky.

An evening of speeches and songs.
A lady who was born at the beginning of the century.
A field full of wild-flowers.

Oh Mr. Harris hears the voice of destiny.
To take the cheese across the wine-dark sea to Her Majesty.

A brief tour of Saratoga. The local reporter shows me around. No, I've never been here before. Every been to Ingersoll? – perhaps some day. All the places and people he wants me to know and to see. What a wonderful community – I see nothing detrimental – every lamp-post and every flower. The reporter is rightly proud of all we survey. I make a few notes as we take a break for a cup of tea.

I sigh the lack of many a thing I sought.

Should I be disturbed, I wonder? Perhaps so – perhaps not. I carry a paper and a pencil with me wherever I go. Inspiration is like lightning – it can find you wherever you are. This is a lovely little city – I am enjoying our little tour. Perhaps what this city lacks – perchance – is abrasive grit. I have not had a poetic thought since I have arrived.

He was drawn towards the paper. He was drawn towards the pen. Had the urge to turn his heart-blood into ink. Read of Homer – read of Chapman. Wrote of both of them, and also Cortez, though by mistake.

"Hear he's writing a great big poem."
"Lots of lines – lots of rhymes – lots of words."

I approach the top of the staircase! Each step has been a cloud! The stairway leads to the sun! The sun is warm and golden above the clouds! I will spend the rest of my life on the sun!

Only the taste - the great undertaking - words are spoken - head is whirling round - attempting to take stock - where i come in - paces off the distance - eyes of all the world - two minuscule lines - there can be no doubt.

So a rhyme might be a rhyme but not apply. The word was 'incandescent'. 'Effervescent'? – 'quiescent'? – 'obsolescent '? – only one of these might suit the work of art.

Well actually, there would be two. Two words to make a couplet. Two words in two sentences in order to make a rhyme.

A couplet, you see, is two sentences that rhyme.

The circle
touched the line.

The fishing boat rose and fell with the water. The fishermen hauled in the catch. Net after net was almost empty. The haul was disappointing today. Where – in the vast of this ocean – were the fish?

We see into the life of things.

Has anyone ever considered that the moon might well be content to be a moon. And that the sun might be discontent to be a sun. And whether the two of them should sit down to talk this through.

The books he read were the words on gravestones. Roles of parchment in forgotten old trunks. An ancient Bible in which the pictures served for words. Ancient writings in old oaken chests. Laid there centuries ago by ancient hands.

Ready for the big adventure.
Pencil, paper and expertise.

How soon hath time, the subtle thief of youth,
Stolen on his wing my three and twentieth year!
My hasting days fly on with full career,
But my late spring no bud or blossom sheweth.
Perhaps my semblance might deceive the truth,
That I to manhood am arrived so near,
And inward ripeness doth much less appear
That some more timely happy spirits indueth.
Yet be it less or more, or soon or slow,
It shall be still in strictest measure even
To that same lot however mean or high,
Toward which time leads me and the will of heaven.
All is, if I have grace to use it so,
As ever in my great taskmaster's eye.

Thorns in the pathway - all bits and pieces - to try to establish - what is the choice - your role as scribe - centre of his own being - assessment of the battle-field - a paucity of information - stand unrivalled - be the same man.

A couplet is two. Two sentences side-by-side. Two concepts – two topics – two ideas.
A couplet is one. Two aspects of a single theme. A double-idea.
The sentences are the wood and the rhyme, you see, is the glue.

Both horses
must pull
in the same direction.

Writing an article on Saragtoga after scouting around the town. 'What a lovely place to spend an afternoon. The natural spring spa, the tree-lined streets, the historic battlefield, the bloom-filled gardens, the charming shops and the porches with swings. What a wonderful place to live. Everything is bright as a top, as clear as a fountain, as kind as a smile. If you love living in Ingersoll you would love it here.'
It seemed no force could wake him from his place.
I have often felt that I could live almost anywhere. Oh the landscapes differ of course, and the climates and the languages vary from place to place. Even the local customs are many and exotic. But people – it seems to me – are the same everywhere. The basic needs – water and food. The need to belong – community and religion – to be one of the herd. And the need – at times – to elevate the thoughts. Where we come from and what our purpose is in life. One can be human and still live anywhere in the world. I could live here – I am sure that I could – though to be 'an American' would seem a little odd.

If the fields should yield in abundance, I would prepare a banquet for you.

On beds of down they did not lie

Thorns on the pathway of life.
A poet whose name is writ in water.
A deep sound striking a knell.

And frugally their goods did buy,

Are you proud of what you've accomplished?
A man of stature – would you say – in this town?
Is there anywhere else you would rather live?

Their one luxury around their door
A few choice flowers their garden bore,

On the other side of the fishing boat. A school of fish hovered just beneath the surface. The school of fish watched as the fishermen plied their trade. They watched the fishermen as they hauled their nets from the water. They knew that soon the fishing boat would sail away.

Roll on thou deep and dark blue ocean! – roll!

Settling down in my hotel. A very charming establishment. Modern gas-light in the room, so I can read. Bright and early I'll be at the fairgrounds to scout, but the judging will be later in the day. A day to have a little look around. Take the temperature of the water – sound the depths of whatever I see. Make a few notes for future articles – visit the seven-thousand pound cheese. I am told that an all-night guard has been posted, so all will be sound.

Chapter 5
Saratoga 2

What an effusion of opulent bliss! What an effervescent irruption of ingenuity in its prime! The Mammoth Cheese stands revealed! The Venus of the cheese-world emerging from her shell. Here at the exhibition pavilion for all to see. A great day for Saratoga – a great day for Ingersoll. Hands across the border – firmly clasped. A burst of applause as the Ingersoll cheese takes pride-of-place.

We are dependant creatures all.

How often is perfection without a flaw? How often do we see the sun without a cloud? The greatest characters in the greatest stories have that within which drags them down. How wonderful to see a cheese with no tragic flaw. A piece of cheese to thrill the ages. A piece of cheese – from Ingersoll – without a marr.

I'm always

A cheese-box sealed in a railway car.
Something nibbling at a swimmer's toes.
A flag pole falling in the midst of battle.

polishing a poem

Are you aware of the epic techniques?
Of the way to tell an epic story?
Do you have a plan to start 'en medias res'?

which I have written.

A dewdrop sparkling in the sun.
A city on the banks of a river.
Baskets of grapes and peaches.

What brought me to Canada is an interesting consideration. 'Circumstances' is the word that I would say. I came here, to Canada, at fourteen years old. Not much for me there, I would avow. Hard work produces nothing, I thought to myself. A bandana with all my wordly goods. Farewell to the folks at home. And off I was to seek a newer world.

And higher yet it still will rise.

Writing is the opening-up of your mind. It is the trepanning of your head. It is the lifting-off of the cap of your skull. It is the looking-down at what is deep inside. This is the mechanism of the writing of a poem.

Becoming a noble. Inheriting an abbey. Running through life on deformed limbs. Wicked and selfish like his uncle. Living in luxury without a dime to his name.

Who hath prophetic vision sees
In future times a ten-ton cheese.
Several companies could join
To furnish curd for great combine.
More honour far than making gun
Of mighty size and many a ton.

"He's designed a new rocking-chair that's supposed to cure the back-ache."
"There's an amazing amount of talent in that man."

Shakespeare and I holding the horses outside the theatre. Two young whippersnappers trying to get a foot in the door. He is adjusting the strap on a bag of oats. "Out of all the young would-be dramatists, James, who are flooding into London, I would estimate that you and I stand the best chance of becoming what we were both of us meant to be."

What they originally had - now is not the time - a piece of wreckage - paths lead upward - a palace and a prison - character as a force - today is a departure - judges' distorted logic - we need sustenance - an agony of pain.

So – what is a working day for me? I have a hobby and I have a trade. My hobby is work, but I don't call it work – what I call work I assume you would call 'my trade'.

I am a carpenter by trade. I built the house we live in now. My second wife and I.

I also built the first, but felt it best to make a fresh start. The first house is still standing. An older couple lives in it now – which would have been the case if my first wife had not died.

The answers were twins

whose mother
could barely tell them apart.

A major mystery. A major stop-gap. A major diversion on this great quest. A meeting is called by the judges. An 'emergency meeting' is called at a critical hour. All of the captains of this great enterprise are called to attend. The press is banned – as I am told when I reach the door.

It seems to be a race for life.

Well – Mr. Harris would actually be, of course, the admiral. The other gentlemen of the factories would be the captains, I am sure. The workers among us – from the cheese factories – those who are here, in Saratoga, and those who are not – would be the crew. Not an armada, of course, as we have come by train.

There was a lady who was dead. Left a book with great ideas. Also left behind a daughter. So he married the daughter instead. Carried on her work in changing humankind.

Machine it could be made with ease
That could turn this monster cheese.
The greatest honour to our land
Would be this orb of finest brand.
Three hundred curd they would need squeeze
For to make this mammoth cheese.

The Mammoth Cheese in all its glory.
Saratoga and Ingersoll.

Shakespeare and I in an empty tavern. We have taken a stroll along the bank of the Thames. He doesn't want the others to overhear. "I have the first line, James, but I'm not sure how the rest of it should go. 'To be or not to be – that is the question.'" He takes a quill and sharpens the end and offers it to me. He pushes the ink-pot across the table and places a piece of clean paper in front of me. "Here – let's see what the two of us can do."

His own little world - a dream and a wisp - promised to capture - a question for you - just the right time - a single figure - should have gone - no fitting category - the same or different - an exception will be made.

I also built a new workshop. Showroom in front – manufactory behind. I built it after the flood and after the fire.

The showroom is my home-away-from-home. I love to show people around. I stand out on the sidewalk and say hello.

When things are not busy, I write a poem. A poem as a means of promotion – a poem about the store. People tell me they look forward to reading my poems.

And interestingly enough,
both rivers reached the sea
at about the same time.

It all started, one could say, with a single cow. Hiram and Lydia Ranney built up their herd. In the beginning they were just two pioneers. Ploughed the land and planted seed and milked the cow. Gradually, they built up a huge herd. Had to hire other people to milk the cows.
To advance to the borders.
The poetic effusion for the day – jotted quickly on the counter-top at the store – is an advertisement of the wonders of our enchanting emporium:

A maiden cried, "Alas!
With horror I'll expire,
Unless you bring me
That true glass
I bought of McIntyre."

So British lands could confederate
Three hundred provinces in one state,
When all in harmony agrees
To be pressed in one like this cheese.
Then one skillful hand could acquire
Power to move the British Empire.

A newspaper with a story of dreadful news.
Premises which are high and dry and safe.
Two people meeting in a choir.

The memories that I treasure are as a roadway over a bridge.

More precious than honey from the bees,
As mentioned in Aristophanes.

Will you call on help from your muse?
State the theme and then proceed?
Use epithets like "rosy-fingered dawn' and 'wine-dark sea'?

Humans can talk and write in imagery and prose.

A Comedy in Five Acts, so please you,

With songs and witticisms to enthuse you,

Children were playing – hens were laying – everything rhymed with every-thing else.

Think of growing wings and you will grow them. Think of growing hooves and they will appear. Think of neither and you will be human the rest of your life.

Steamships sailing up and down.
The haze above Niagara Falls.
The walls of an undefended fortress.

Oh Mr. Harris is a man of noble carriage.
He would make for Queen Victoria an excellent second marriage.

The mystery takes a backward step. The Ingersollians sense a crime. The captains stand on the steps of the music gazebo and explain. There is no category - we are told - so the judges say - for 'the biggest cheese in the competition' - none of the other behemoths has entered - as of this hour - if there are any - that is to say - if there are any such massive cheeses - they have failed to apply. I am wondering why the admiral doesn't appear.
Child's happiness knows no alloy.
The Mammoth Cheese is a bee laden with honey. The Mammoth Cheese is a laden bee without a hive. Nature always provides – humans often fall short in their aims. Are the judges wearing blind-folds? How could the judges not see that honey must have a hive?

Setting his chair outside on the lawn. Pen and paper close at hand. Having some thoughts about a nightingale. Capturing sentiments in words. Oh to fly along with the nightingale above the sky.

But various curds must be combined,
And each factory their curd must grind,
To blend harmonious in one
This great cheese of mighty span,
And uniform in quality
A glorious reality.

"First thing I look for in the newspaper."
"Always look for an advertisement dressed up as a poem."

A note from a very close friend. Shakespeare is having trouble with his new play. His spelling has not improved, but I squint and peruse. I meet him at the dock. "I call it 'the sandbag scene', James. It is not going well. You were always chock-full with ideas. Dramatic to your finger-tips. Could you come up with another way to have her die?" We take a water-taxi across the Thames. "I'll have to think about this for a while, Will. If I get an idea, perhaps I'll rough out the whole scene. It will have something to do with putting out a light."

The traces of blood - to peer inside - rivulet from that stream - just a shepherd - defeat the combatants - bear much thinking about - make me pay - brings no gloom - conceal the dawn - game without a prize.

The furniture workshop is out the back. I call it 'the manufactory'. It's a maze of saws and lathes and belts and pulleys.

We bring in the timbers. We cut them to size. We saw them into boards.

We cut out the pieces for each piece of furniture and glue them together. Sand and finish – we do the whole process all right there. Then we move them out to the showroom and put them on sale.

Did the paths converge
or did they diverge?

The dangers of speculative speculation, I often warn myself. Something a cow in the field would never do. Best not to speculate is what I often tell myself. Only speculate on that which you already know.

Then this thought you can advance.

Sitting on the back porch in the morning. A pencil and paper and a cup of tea.

Once, while digging 'neath the snow,
'Mid Canadian winter, lo!
To our joy and surprise,
We saw some violets in full bloom
Gazing at us with loving eyes,
Thanking us for opening their tomb.

Moving to London to find a patron. Moving to London to make his way. His way was barred by the walls of indifference. His was the way of mangled hope and lost despair. Lie down in the streets and starve to death for all we care.

But it will need a powerful press
This cheese queen to caress,
And a large extent of charms
Hoop will encircle in its arms,
And we do not now despair,

But we shall see it at world's fair.

Confusion in Saratoga.
A desire to sort things out.

We love cold water as it flows from the fountain,
Which nature hath brewed alone in the mountain,
In the wild woods and in the rocky dell
Where man hath not been but the deer love to dwell,
And away across the sea in far distant lands
In Asia's gloomy jungles and Africa's drifting sands,
Where to the thirsty traveller a charming spot of green
Is by far the rarest gem his eyes have ever seen.
And when he hath quenched his thirst at the cooling spring,
With many grateful songs he makes the air to ring.
For many nights he dreams of this scene of bliss,
And when he thinks of Heaven it is of such as this.

*Tickle a swimmer's toes - one burnt out - squeezing a clod - there's other
things - a decent into the underworld - found by others - smouldering inside
the head - it would be best - just find the means - drifting down a river.*

I don't let anyone go back there – to the workshop. I used to – but no longer
do. You could call it a safety concern, I suppose.

Lots of people would like to see it. When we opened our new store, we had
a sign. 'This Way to See the Manufactory.'

But now it's something I discourage for the customers. Only my workers go
back there now. It's all lathes and belts and pulleys and plenty of noise.

Both horses
must pull
at the same time.

The swelling of the throng. The music-gazebo is alive and buzzing. The
word finds every Canadian ear on the exhibition grounds. Every Ingersollian
is attuned to the gaping wound. An arrow through the heart or a blow on the
thigh. The Ingersoll-leaders explain the plight. They explain it over and over
as more arrive. Opinions given – opinions received. Have we been led into an
ambush? Was this the slaughter of the three hundred at Thermopylae all along?
Were we too trusting? – too Canadian? – too polite for our own good? Why is
there is no category for the biggest cheese ever wrought?
May you take deep root.
What is a competition without a competition? What is an accomplishment
without an accomplishment-prize? What is a light if it is placed beneath a

bushel? Logic is logic no matter what – no matter what country – no matter what clime – no matter what principle is at stake or what the prize. The judges must think on another level. The judges must put themselves in our place. The judges must think as Ingersollians – put their Saratogan pettiness behind.

And view the people all agog, so
Excited o'er it in Chicago.
To seek fresh conquests Queen of Cheese
She may sail across the seas,
Where she would meet reception grand
From the warm hearts in old England.

If all I had was a crust of bread and a glass of water, I would share my sustenance with you.

But never hoped to own the soil

The number of words in the Iliad.
A handful of wild-flowers in a vase.
A squirrel who gathers nuts.

But serve as hinds to sweat and toil,

No doubt, of course, you will write your epic in verse?
Can you write rhyming couplets by the yard?
Can you manage twenty-four books of clever rhymes?

To work and toil for him had charm
He hoped some day to own a farm,

Hard to imagine having a town without a river. Though of course you could have a river without a town. They just seem to go together – though of course the words don't rhyme. Perhaps in another language – maybe in Sanscrit or Urdu or some of those other tongues. If I'd stayed in Scotland, I'd probably be rhyming in Gaelic by now. What is the Gaelic, I wonder, for 'river'? – the Gaelic for 'town'?

Round many lips a sneer of serious doubt did lurk.

"What, you might well ask, are the qualities that make for poetry of the highest order? And what, we may also ask, are the qualities that identify poetry which has, alas, fallen well below that mark? The story of this Janus-faced inquiry – this double-sided, gold-and-leaded coin – would doubtless be rewarded by the inclusion in the discussion of the latest offering of poesy from the Bard of Ingersoll, James McIntrye."

Chapter 6
Saratoga 3

Another emergency meeting – 'Emergency Meeting Number Two'. The judge's decisions, we are told, are always final. But an exception will be made in this particular case. We are guests, so we are told, and must be accorded full respect. Another chance to present the logic of the Ingersoll-concern. Once again the press is barred. Sealed lips – sealed doors – sealed minds?

Such is the fond illusion of my heart.

'Emergency Meeting Number Two'? – or 'Number Three'? Let's see now – there was the meeting that caused the great concern – the judges, the admiral and the captains. Then the meeting of explanation at the music-gazebo – our leaders offered to pay for the damage to the flower-beds; the Ingersollians meant no harm; however the throng was very large and it was hard to make one's point without crowding around – so this would be – let me get my note-book out – 'Emergency Meeting Number Three'.

Or perhaps

The asking of an incidental question.
The unveiling of a spectacular block of cheese.
A guessing-game without a prize.

I am writing a poem

Why the interest in furniture-making?
Why did you apprentice in that trade?
Was it planned or did it just fall into your lap?

on a new idea.

A Christmas tree laden with fruit.
A stage carrying passengers and mail.
The planning of an entirely new town.

What are the thoughts that I have never known? The thoughts that chase each other around in the cold-cellar of my mind? The thoughts that lurk in the misty valleys we cannot see? If I met them, what would I do? Would I embrace them, turn and run, or draw my sword?

Stone walls do not a prison make.

A candle has and endless supply of light locked inside. Light a candle and let the light come pouring out.

Falling in love and yearning madly. Writing poems of hope and despair. Boxing, riding, gambling, drinking. Quaffing liquor from a skull. Applying the whip to the foaming hide of the horse of life.

"Came here as a boy."
"Worked his way up."

We are drifting down a river! The forest is dark on either side! Fires are burning to the left on the hillside! There is chanting to a drum! 'Hate the heart! – love the brain!'

Heavy, dark, profound - a big black void - that is the fact - every name written down - into the waves - new and alien landscape - make our mark - the waters plunge - forces that hurt - the water at the well.

What is my role? A very probing question. The most general question tends to generate the most detailed response.

Well – everyone has a number of roles. A number of roles in the universe. A number of roles in time.

I am a husband. I was a father. I am a member of a lodge.

The distance between these two points
must never vary.

No light whatsoever. There is no light, whatsoever, in the judges' eyes. Each one takes a small wedge of cheese from the offering on the plate. Each one lifts it – with his hand – to his mouth. Actually, one of the judges is a female – one female out of three – but she is equally inscrutable as she chews.

My shaping sprit of imagination.

Do females – by their nature – in their minds, their hearts, their souls – know more or less than a man would know about cheese? That Queen Victoria is a female is well-known. One judge makes use of a glass of water – is that a good sign? The other two wave away the proffered glass – what does that mean? The tension mounts as the clock is ticking. The judges stand and slowly chew the Ingersoll cheese.

Sent his poems to a great poet. Hoped to be welcomed to the club. Never heard a word in response. The great man never cut a page. Is an unread poem dead or just asleep?

A failure to reach an agreement.
Watching the judges eat.

We are drifting down a river! The forest is dark on either side! Fires are burning to the right on the hillside! There is chanting to a drum! 'Hate the brain! – love the heart!'

A homecoming of sorts - a blank page - it floated away - made a prominent mark - a mysterious shore - an effervescent irruption - the question then - to have a look - never think in prose - the stab to the heart.

I am a designer of furniture. I am a salesman who explains the wonders of the show-room floor.

I was an excellent father. As good as I knew how to be. I wiped tears away and soothed the nighttime fears.

I am an excellent coffin-maker. I make an excellent pine box. I am an obituary writer – and an undertaker too.

Two burley fellows
played
at tug-of-war.

The boy looked down at the water in the well. It was a well where he had spent many a day. The boy had a penny in his pocket. He leaned over and looked at the water in the well. He wondered whether it was a wishing well.

What the hand dare seize the fire.

You are also fond of books? I might have known. The lending-library is quite a coup for our little town.

Letters refusing to settle on a page.
Every lamppost and every flower.
A bill collector knocking on a door.

The memories that are painful are as a fire or a raging flood.

Pipes were played and sung were odes
About the ambrosia of the gods.

Do you think of yourself as creative?

The kind of person who deals in ideas?
The kind who is always making something new?

Angels think only in imagery.

As acted upon our stage at London,
With all the talent that you have come to count on.

He conceived of a mammoth project that would take him to the heights.

Hear the snow on the mountain. Hear the rain on the ground. To hear your-self you would need to grow a third ear.

Lines written in a quotation album.
A field of yellow golden grain.
A poet writing poems about his home.

Puzzling out the structure of my epic poem.
If a block of cheese sets out on a voyage, and there must be something that it is seeking, and it cannot be seeking itself – the block of cheese – then it fol-lows that the hero of the poem cannot, of course, be the block of cheese.

Second place is the shattering news! Second place is the stab to the heart! Second place in 'The Taste Competition'! How could anyone be deaf to the voice of the Ingersoll Cheese?
Christ that my love were in my arms and I in my bed again.
What did he say?, people whisper. Is he reading from the wrong card? Sure-ly there must be a mistake! Not a cow in the world can match an Ingersoll cow!

Seeing the marbles in the museum. Writing of love both found and lost. Heifers lowing and young girls running. Young boys chasing them round a vase. If only we had immortality like the gods.

"See him sittin' down at the bridge on the bench."
"That's where he gets the inspiration for his poems."

We are drifting on a river! Fires are burning on each bank! There is chant-ing left and right! There is the sound of roaring water! We dare not light a torch!

O'er cropped the weary land - what to convey - arms around the whole
world - unconsidered-information - based on nothing - hard to tell - - i am ask-
ing myself - i would guess - have that within - seeing the reality.

Roles change. Roles diverge. Roles collide.

I have had roles that I have yearned for and never had a sniff. I have had roles that I have attained and lost again. I've seen myself as a loose collection – a moth-eaten bag – of rag-tag roles.

I've had roles thrust upon me. And roles I have thrust aside. I've had roles I have wrestled with in the slimiest swamps.

The Ancient Egyptians took medicine
to a very high level.

The boy looked down at the water in the well. It was a well where he had spent many a day. His grandpa had told him that it was a wishing well. He had dropped a penny a day into the well for a week. Now he wondered whether the well was a wishing well.

Sudden a thought came like a full-blown rose.

I am fortunate in my employees. The manufactory runs itself. I draw designs and then the rest is smooth as glass.

Starving in a garret. Not a crumb to eat all day. Hungry for books, not meat and potatoes. Ink and paper were his mainstay. He ate with his eyes, not with his mouth.

Disappointment in Saratoga.
A somber train ride home.

In Xanadu did Kubla Khan
A stately pleasure-dome decree:
Where Alph, the sacred river, ran
Through caverns measureless to man
Down to a sunless sea.
So twice five miles of fertile ground
With walls and towers were girdled round:
And here were gardens bright with sinuous rills,
Where blossomed many an incense-bearing tree;
And here were forests ancient as the hills,
Enfolding sunny spots of greenery.

Serve for any topic - my ship goes down - not open to the world - forces that help - off to the side - rendered into print - paths lead downward - running through life - to label each piece - ate with his eyes.

Yes, I have assumed many roles. Many, many roles. In what role will I be judged when I stand before God?

Did we get to choose our roles? What will God do if we refuse to talk? How can we talk our way into heaven if our lips are sealed?

About undertaking I shall simply refuse to talk. There was a young boy who was dragged by a horse – an ankle caught and the horse ran away and dragged the boy for miles. Usually, you sew them up, but in his case, there was not enough to sew.

Two wise men spoke
at the same time.

Loading the cheese-box on the train. A dreary day in Saratoga. A dreary day – for sure – in Ingersoll. Tired and exhausted – eyes downcast – the weary Ingersollians board the home-bound train. A long ride home and some sober second-thought.

And thus the heart will break, yet brokenly live on.

A Jason without the Golden Fleece – the Augean stables not flushed clean as they were in the tale. How write an article for the newspaper in which the expected did not come to happen? About a non-event in which nothing happened at all? My pencil worries the paper to no avail.

Not a thought in my head. Not a thought anywhere in the spaces of my head.

So he hired with Reuben Tripp

A leaf talking to a root.
A poet who writes a silly poem.
A meeting at the Douglas Hotel.

The wealthiest man in the township.

Do you recall your first furniture design?
You'd rather design than work in the shop?
Does it give you the same satisfaction as writing verse?

Tripp's only child, his daughter Jane,
He sought her love and not in vain,

He leaned over and looked down at the water. It was a well where he had spent many a day. He wondered if it was a wishing well. The boy clutched the penny in his hand. What, he wondered, would he do with the penny today.

In what torn ship soever I embark.

What is the difference between A and B? What is the difference between A and Z? Between the beginning of the alphabet and the middle? – between the middle and the end? Saratoga – Toronto – Hamilton. London – Paris – the entire world. The greatest journey, they say, begins with a single step. The greater journey, I say, begins with a backwards step. What is the letter that comes before 'A' in the alphabet?

Chapter 7
Ingersoll 4

The newspaper office in Ingersoll. Slamming my article – defiantly – on the counter. Not bothering to ask if this is the office of the *New York Times*. 'The triumph in New York is not unmitigated. A tiny technical glitch was allowed to interfere. The fact that only one mammoth cheese had seen fit to enter the competition struck the judges' distorted logic in such an illogical way as that no fitting category could possibly be devised. Since when has it been a crime to be one-of-a-kind?'

A brother looked at me as though I had been Cain.

Reeling. Attempting to take stock. Not of the store, but of the trip to Saratoga. What was the purpose of the trip? – what was lost and what was gained? An assessment of the battlefield after a skirmish. What is the definition of 'a strategy', 'a tactic', 'a campaign'?

It's not a case

The coughing of blood on a handkerchief.
A doctor who is overwhelmed by snow.
A gradual awakening to life's possibilities.

of getting away

What would the landscape be in your poem?
Will it have epic stature and epic size?
The sky, the sea, the land – the underworld?

from life.

A stack of firewood ready for winter.
Flatboats moving in a canal.
A young lady rowing a boat.

I am a cabinet-maker by trade. Saw – chisel – drawknife – plane. Everything else flows from that. Maker of furniture – maker of coffins – proprietor of a furniture-emporium. Everything else I am is a rivulet from that stream.

His high deeds are all in vain.

Writing a poem is like squeezing a clod of earth. Writing a poem is like squeezing a piece of the sky. Writing a poem is like squeezing a handful of water. Writing a poem is like squeezing a flame of fire. When you are squeezing as hard as you can, you are writing a poem.

A tour of the continent. Many adventures and many affairs. Writing a poem that captured the moment. Standing in Venice on the Bridge of Sighs. A palace and a prison on each hand.

"He was apprenticed to old Frazer."
"He learned the trade like a cracker-jack."

My friend Byron does not praise lightly. "Of my poem, '*Childe Harold*', James, as you know, I am justifiably proud. A superior literary feat – to be sure – to be sure. But the poem that you wrote, James, as we chased ourselves around Europe, was a better poem, I have to admit, by far. Too bad it was swept away when we crossed that raging ford.'

Divide yourself in two - swept the bridges away - calling for justice - proclaims the fact - done all he could - have we run aground - for all to see - ragtag roles - a thought is an idea - assumed many roles.

So what are the ingredients – the check-list – the items in a recipe – for an epic adventure? That is the question that I often ask of myself. What are the key – the essential – elements in such an enterprise?

Is it the same as everyday life? Is it reserved for exceptional beings in exceptional times? Are these two experiences the same or different at the innermost core?

It seems to me that it starts as an everyday story – an ordinary story, as it were – and then gradually there arises a philosophical quandary – a missing idea. To go on a journey in search of the special idea that is missing in the everyday life. To find that missing idea and bring it home.

If it did they would be
two different points in time.

Organizing the displays. I've been neglecting the store of late. Moving the easy-chairs closer to the door. I want the elderly to have a shorter walk. Put a sign inviting all to 'Have a Seat'. Once they sit in one of these, we'll have our sale. There was a gentleman, one day, who fell asleep. I should have offered to pay him to come here every day.

When fairies danced upon the green.

It is hard to see the logic. Though I try – though I try. The Mammoth Cheese is a mammoth cheese. The Mammoth Cheese was exhibited in New York. There was no other mammoth cheese present – or even rumoured to be extant in that or in any other United State. Hence – ergo – it must follow – that the Ingersoll Mammoth Cheese was the biggest mammoth cheese in the competition at Saratoga, New York. That is the fact and only the fact. So why – then – was it not awarded a prize?

Feeling battered. Feeling bruised. Why write poems that no one reads? Clouds were covering up the sunshine. If this is summer, can winter be far behind?

The news from New York.
Taking stock in Ingersoll.

My Lord Byron is in his cups. The candles gutter and flicker and fade. "Your ghost story, James – the one that you told that night. 'Twas a story that put the rest of us in the shade. If envy is sin, then 'guilty' am I. Too bad it floated away on the scum of that foul-smelling bog." Our glasses clink loudly as the curtains conceal the dawn.

No longer have any idea - not a topic - asked for the recipe - assaulted the brain - they made adjustments - a question which generates - have to consider - have a plan - neglected the daily chores - did not come to happen.

A journey to the ends of the earth. A journey to far-flung lands. A commitment to a mind-shaping experience, though the trek might be dangerous and far.

Raging rivers, crashing rocks, pounding surf. Blazing sun, ferocious cold, forbidding terrain. Never to falter, never to flag, never to fail.

Find the gem. Find the amethyst. Find the pearl.

Every try was
a stale-mate –
nothing moved.

Lydia Ranney figured it out. How to turn the milk into cheese. How to make more than their family could consume. How to sell it in the dry-goods store. The best type of cheddar cheese. Mr. Harris was a little later on the scene.

They made strong efforts for to fly.

Am I British or am I Canadian? The uninformed might ask. I am as large as the world I inhabit. Putting my arms around the whole world as I write my poems.

But let it never be forgot
That distant hills, when closer seen,
Are after all a barren spot –
Not like your own hills, clad in green.

A stream flowing into another stream.
Balboa discovering the Pacific, or maybe Cortez.
People who cast themselves on the waters.

My thoughts, at times, are as a heart devoid of blood.

While listening Greeks would sit and chew
The product of the goat and ewe.
The greatest cheese from Greece is feta.
Homer used to eat a lot of

Will it contain the supernatural?
Forces that help and forces that hurt?
The occasional raging tempest or friendly breeze?

Angels never think in prose.

And I must add, before I forget,
That the plot would hinge on a cheese omelette.

He would write an epic poem on a huge cheese.

Drink the light and you will shine. Drink the dark and you will fade. Drink
neither light nor dark and you will starve.

Children falling into a mill-race.
A flock of birds flying overhead.
A farmer with two sturdy cows.

Oh Mr. Harris is the leader of the quest.
He always has the ideas that are the best.

'Toronto' is the word on everyone's lips. They murmur it as bees throughout the town. The ashes of the Phoenix calling for justice. 'Saratoga' is barely
mentioned – murmured with lowered voice. Better it be forgotten as a word. A
hand reaching up to a calendar and pausing at a page. 'Saratoga, New York' are
the date and the time. The hand ponders and then tears the page away.
He was afraid that he would drown.

Why no category of 'The Largest Cheese'? Were all the Americans afraid to enter? Do they only make miniature cheeses down there? That young reporter asked for the recipe – no doubt that would have been his 'scoop' for the day. He talked with his mouth full as he was wolfing a plate of it down. Are the Americans still smarting over the shellacking they took in the war of 1812? – when the British lion took a birch rod to the upstart cub? Is this a form of sour-grapes revenge? I told him you can't make Ingersoll cheese without Ingersoll cows.

Wrote of autumn – lovely autumn. Wrote of the barn and the threshing floor. Wrote of the field and the sun and the harvest. Made you feel as if you were there. Of the bursting of the grape on the roof of your tongue.

"That new store is something special."
"He always greets you at the door."

"Now that is an order!" Lord Byron shouts, as loud as his croaking voice can sound. He brushes the mosquito-netting aside with a feeble hand. "I charge you, James, I charge you! No sense two of us dying here in this fearful hole! One of us has to carry the standard! – one of us has to lead the charge! Promise me you will fight with your pen and not with your sword!"

Tell accurate time - a chain with two links - open up a skull - no one's business - t'was but the wind - changing places with yourself - on an individual basis - running through life - pretty-well restored - what is the difference.

Every epic needs a hero. A wily and courageous man. A bold adventurer who plunges into threatening seas.
A spark in the mind and a glint in the eye. Rippling muscles and sun-bronzed skin. A leader who leads his charges through the gates of hell.
Or does it have to be a human? What is the role of the Golden Fleece? Can an epic hero be a piece of cheese?

They could open up a skull
and look inside.

The dangers of speculative speculation. Especially the backwards-looking kind. Like trying to look at the past through a crystal ball. The past is a barn-door left open. The past will never go away if you don't close it shut.
Who did believe each fairy tale.
Scanning the newspaper and reacting to the dreadful news in rhyme:

At London, Thames is a broad stream
Which was the scene of a sad theme.

A fragile steamer there did play
O'ercrowded on a Queen's birthday.

Writing more than the clock has minutes. Writing more than the clock has
hours. Handing his squibs to the journal editors. Handed pennies for labours of
work. Gratitude to him was a dead dog in the street.

Pressing ahead on the journey.
Things will be different from now on.

In summer time it doth seem good
To seek the shade of the green wood,
For it doth banish all our care
When we gaze on scene so fair.
And birds do here in branches sing
So merrily in early spring,
And lovingly they here do pair,
Their mutual joys together share.
Here nature's charming never rude,
Inspiring all with happy mood,
Tables had choice fruit of season,
And we too had feast of reason.
With joy at night each one did gaze
At the mighty bonfire's blaze;
The tree leaves shone like silver bright,
The lanterns too, were pleasing sight.

Without these disasters - topics that are waiting - made a life for themselves
- backwards-looking kind - ask a simple question - out of a book - i would es-
timate - the crest of a wave - my watch insists - an empty cart.

So what do I have to work with? What information do I have? Can an epic
be written that starts in Ingersoll?
A group of owners pool their factories. They gather milk from eight hundred cows. They devise a method of making a mammoth cheese.
And that is where I come in – I, the one who wields the pen. I gather the
information. I turn the information into words.

Each had his own soap box
at Speakers' Corner.

An interview with Mr. Harris – the admiral of the fleet. A request for an
assessment of the quest. I see the man – I hear him speak. But when is an interview not an interview?

We did but quickly stand amazed.

Now is not the time, Mr. McIntyre, for an interview. Though I respect your role as scribe of this event. I have Saratoga-poison choking my veins. Now is definitely not the time for an interview. The words that I am feeling should definitely not be rendered into print.

Not a thought in my head. Not a thought anywhere in the spaces of my head. Not a thought in any of the crevices or cracks in any of the corners of my cranium.

As Jacob served for Rachel dear

A poet trying an epic for the first time.
Managing to find the appropriate rhymes.
A question as to who is speaking the words.

So John he served year after year,

Profound adventures – heroic deeds?
Every character as a force that is found in life?
A test of physical and mental attributes?

Till rich enough to buy bush farm
For to chop down with his strong arm.

Spending some time with my wife. I've been neglecting her of late. Spending hours at the store – off on the quest of the mammoth cheese. Taking a handful of wild-flowers home to put in a vase. Found them growing beside the bench by the river-side. Did Odysseus bring home flowers to put in a vase?
I wished to cross to the other shore.
"It is often said that the mark of genius is that a single figure stands alone on a promontory and peers far off in the distance of his particular area of expertise, seeing the future of his fellow humans in a way that none of those on the ground can possibly perceive or even contemplate. If his view of the future of the art of poetry is indicative of the future, then James McIntyre will be hailed, by those not yet alive, as the harbinger of the poetic mills of future gods."

Chapter 8
Toronto 1

On the train bound for Toronto. Bearing a larger Ingersoll contingent than travelled to the earlier town. Most have been to the Toronto Exhibition many times. This time, though, there's a personal Ingersoll-stake. Toronto's exhibition is the biggest exhibition in Ontario, for sure – a worthy host for all the agricultural wonders of the age.

The albatross fell off and sank.

But Ingersoll – little Ingersoll – not so prominent as Toronto on the map of Ontario – on the map of Canada – on the map of the globe – is the birthplace of the biggest cheese in all the world.

It's not

An elder bee telling secrets to younger bees.
The airing of linen on a line.
A lighthouse that reveals both rocks and shoals.

an escape

How long have you been a poet?
How many poems have you composed?
Do you plan to publish them in a book someday?

or a mental holiday.

A boy out shooting for quail.
A doctor struggling through drifts of snow.
A church concert with speeches and poems.

There are currents inside of creeks. There are creeks inside of streams. There are streams inside of rivers. There are rivers inside of oceans. A drop of rain can settle down on the ocean floor.

Full many a glorious morning have I seen.

Born of a dream and a wisp of sunlight. We are carried along on the stream to the ends of the earth.

Plunging into the swirling waters. Daring to swim the Hellespont. Trailing his useless legs behind him. Thinking of rhymes as he braved the waves. This will give me a verse for my poem when I reach shore.

"Don't ever mention his first wife."
"Nor the loss of his boy."

I am taking a tour of myself! Sailing down a river of blood! I am on my way to my heart! The blood is rushing in a torrent! My blood is flowing freely to my heart!

The edge of a cliff - i do the books - carved a home - hopes and dreams and failures - to get to see - after the flood - any other presence - think of the future - to clear the air - best for all concerned.

Am I writing my autobiography? What a strange question to ask. Do I look old to you? – do I look wise?

To put it bluntly – as clear as I can – emphatically 'No!' I am definitely not writing my autobiography. Of my private life I do not intend to write even one word.

I print my poems in ink and on paper. Not on the windows of my house. I don't invite my readers to peer inside.

If it did they would be
two different points in memory.

So where's the launching-place for me? When and where will I take my place on the world stage? Not Saratoga, New York, that is for sure. Dust in the hand on a windy day – I have long ago forgotten to remember that name.
Runs in blood down palace walls.
Certainly Toronto will be the first stage on my literary journey. There's still London – Paris – the world. So where does Toronto fit into all this? Is such a term as 'pre-launching-place' a valid term?

Disillusioned with life in England. Atheist poems didn't sell. Packed his books and his wife and children. Made the trek to a warmer clime. Invited other poets to join him in the sun.

Arriving in Toronto.
A trainload of Ingersollians.

I am taking a tour of myself! I am stranded in my heart! My sail is in the doldrums! There is no wind or wave! The blood leaves in a trickle from my heart!

Hidden meanings to explore - just an idea - a series of questions - two answers contended - every purpose has a glue - tearing apart your soul - abundance of furniture - can talk and write - catch a glimpse - drown my pen.

Look at me closely. What do you see? Do I look like a chunk of mammoth cheese?

I do not own a factory. I own no cows. I make no curds or whey.

Readers will see my ink and my paper. That's as close as they'll get to me. My fingerprints will not appear on the page.

The two fellows thought and talked
as they ate their lunch
and considered
the rope that lay on the ground.

He watched the bucket through the window. The bucket sat on a table. The rain was pelting down. Rivulets formed in the fields. The bucket filled with water to the brim.

At length the man perceives it die away.

Just a nightmare was all it was. Something I've learned to take in stride. Some day the nightmare- need will fade away.

A bridge replacing one that washed away.
Writing in another person's voice.
Two people who form a glue-like bond.

I think of you, sometimes, as a water-droplet an ocean away from me.

Feta, sprinkled on his salad
As he chanted his ancient ballad
Of Achilles and Odysseus, two ever-ready brainy-men,
Who sailed all over the Mediterannean.

Do you have a favourite poem?
Favourite topics about which to write?
Are there topics that you deliberately avoid?

Angels have no need to talk.

Popularity was Shakespeare's chief aim.
So, on that basis, permit me to couple his and my name.

Homer and Milton had immortalized religion and war.

Distinguished for love. Distinguished for war. All those medals on your chest. Pretty soon you'll need a bigger uniform.

A farmer gathering sheaves of golden grain.
A slim volume of occasional poems.
The dreams of a young shepherd boy.

Oh Mr. Harris will take us far across the seas.
Her Majesty the cheese will surely please.

The villages and farms and houses fly quickly by. Chatter of Toronto by the people who crowd the aisles. What time is the judging – I want to be there – but there's other things in Toronto besides the fair. When does the train go back? – I was late once, and had to spend a whole 'nother day. What's the fare at the main gate? – do you pay, again, for the exhibition room?
I saw eternity the other night.
So what can I write about for Toronto? What to convey to the readers of Ingersoll? – those readers who didn't come, that is, to Toronto today? Some of the readers would know this city – some of them wouldn't know Toronto at all. Do I tell my readers it's just like Ingersoll? More streets – more houses – more stores? More people – more dogs – more cats? More of everything that you find in Ingersoll? Is that what my readers want to be told? If I wrote like that would they ask for their money back?

Falling in love with the girl next door. Each was living in half a house. Fanny my love – oh Fanny my love. Nothing have I but my ink and my pen. Oh to be able to join their hearts and have one home.

"Gives very generous to the church."
"Always ready to share what he has."

I am taking a tour of myself! I must explore my brain! I must tour the various levels as Dante would do! Why does the blood flow so freely into my heart? Why does the blood only trickle out again!

A wise precaution - enjoying the sunbeam - pointing the prow - always new paths - what is the price - know what I say - not one effort - there is no category - discussing the faults - just suppose.

I never write my poems about myself. I write my poems in what is called 'imagery'. That is a language that hides the life and reveals the thought.

The hero of my epic, for instance, will not be me. I am not a Greek hero reefing the sails in stormy seas. I do not scramble ashore as my ship goes down.

And when the hero appears in the harbour – ship lost but the quest intact – that will not be my head which is bobbing above the waves.

They named the parts
that were at peace.

The rain eased off. The sun came out from behind the clouds. He went outside and checked the bucket. The bucket was empty and dry. He couldn't detect a hole in the bottom or the sides.

My face in thine eye, thine in mine appears.

The new bridge is made of brick. Anchored deeply into the banks. In the spring the ice would sweep the bridges away.

What to do with his interests? What to do with his burgeoning talent? Acceptance was a door that was barred and then closed. Success was a portcullis that had been raised. Advancement was a moat that was filled with brackish debris.

Ready for the big adventure.
Pencil, paper and expertise.

There was a sound of revelry by night,
And Belgium's capital had gathered then
Her beauty and her chivalry, and bright
The lamps shone o'er fair women and brave men.
A thousand hearts beat happily; and when
Music arose with its voluptuous swell,
Soft eyes looked love to eyes which spake again,
And all went merry as a marriage bell;
But hush! hark! a deep sound strikes like a rising knell!

The size and shape - walking along the path - plunge back into the river - right in your conjecture - puzzled looks - a mighty feat - the deepest level of thought - squint and peruse - reduced to single-bite size - attempt to figure out.

So please, no questions about my life. An uncut book, a locked cupboard, a sealed cave. A beach with only one set of footprints on the sand.

Yes I have had two wives. Yes, I have had a son. The little boy who used to laugh and sing.

But biography is 'out'. Not a topic for this interview. And I shall never write my autobiography.

When they got to heaven each wise man
was asked the same question:

The fate of the Mammoth Cheese will be the fate of my epic. The fate of my epic will be the fate of the Mammoth Cheese.
And like enough thou know'st thy estimate.
A chain with two links – a bird with two wings – a cart with two horses. Neither on top – neither below – working side by side.

My son died in the new shop. It happened after the new bridge was built. After the cleaning up from the flood. After the reconstruction and renewal of our building from the major fire.

He his young oxen did adorn

Two young whipper-snappers trying to get a foot in the door.
An escarpment which is referred to as a mountain.
A person who is wounded by a metaphor.

With fine gay ribbons on each horn,

What is there yet for you to do?
As a writer who captures life in all its array?
Are there topics that are waiting for you to attend?

And to his home with joy and pride
He did bring sweet blooming bride,

The sky clouded over. He looked out the window at the bucket. The rain came down in torrents. Rivulets formed in the ditches. He sat and watched the bucket fill again.
A feeling that I was not for that hour.
The sunlight comes through the windows of the store. I do the books in the early morning by candle-light. Always a thrill each time I open up the door.

Chapter 9
Toronto 2

The Ingersoll crowd surges from the train station. The Ingersoll crowd surges down the street. A small group clusters at the railway car with the Mammoth Cheese. I stay behind to make notes on the unloading.

But soon there came a dismal cry.

Always my eye on the target. Always my mind on the central fact. Never distracted from duty or purpose. Like the jewels in the Tower. Like the gold in the federal mint. In a nondescript railway car sits the Mammoth Cheese.

It's an intense exploration

The posting of an all-night guard.
An unbroken girdle around the globe.
A profession with a very high ladder.

of what I think

Who will be your epic hero?
A man of stature, integrity, grit?
A man who never deviates from his chosen course?

and what I feel.

A memory of three-score years.
A small book lying in the road.
Eating a peck of strong onions.

We have a fine library in town. It was my idea at first. A room with the finest books. A place to have a chat and meet others who like to read. Others took up the cause and now we have our library-room. The little room at the back of the dry-goods store. When my own book is ready, I will place it in the library on the shelf.

Torrent onward rushes frantic.

Writing is attaining double-vision. Writing is looking in through your eyes and out through your eyes at the same time. When you stand on your eye-lids and look both ways, you are writing a poem.

Awakening one morning to find himself famous. Mad and bad and dangerous to know. Dressed in black and refusing to dance. Writing poems that sold like hot-cakes. A man of intrigue, a man of romance.

"Can't figure out what went wrong at Saratoga."
"That's for Mr. Harris to have to figure out."

Trelawny and I gathering driftwood on the beach near Leghorn. Making a funeral-pyre for the body of Shelley – a true friend. Were I not prone to queasiness, I had gone.

What a silly thing - after the fire - think like angels - one that washed away - head off any questions - i have failed - conditions are not propitious - just the right tension - it's a maze - clear spring water.

Do I have a philosophy, you ask. Now that's a pretty big word. 'A philosophy of life', I presume you mean.

Oh I've perused the great philosophers – I have a gigantic book on my shelf. I flip the pages and skim my eye over the words. Hard to make head nor tale of what they say.

But I've done a lot of living. Lived two or three lives, I would say. Been a boy – been a youth – been a man.

*It they were it would be
a different universe.*

Shoulder to shoulder with a dozen Toronto reporters. Here to pounce upon the story of the day. Notebooks sticking out of their pockets – pencils stuck behind their ears. Yawning and scratching and blowing the nose. So smug – so sophisticated – so jaded. Toronto news is Toronto news – news for Ontario at most. Well, here is the news about the news – all the world will soon take note of the Ingersoll Cheese.

How he was oft o'erwhelmed in snow.

A narrow opening in the sliding door of the railway car. Mr. Harris and the other manufacturers slip inside. Waiting – waiting – waiting – my pencil poised to record the official word. Finally, the sliding-door slides open and a voice is heard to cry – No damage! – no damage to the cheese!

A young friend had fallen in battle. Not the battle of the sword, but of the pen. They have tripped-up Adonais. Left him lying in the dirt. Opened his mouth and removed his poetic tongue.

The Mammoth Cheese in all its glory.
Toronto and Ingersoll.

Shelley and I were like two brothers. Shelley and I were like two friends. Shelley and I would always read each other's poems. Now his pen is at the bottom of the sea. All I can think of is Shelley saying that he couldn't wait to see the looks on people's faces on the day that my poems come out in book form.

Or are their scars - not a banner - contemplate my poems - passing on the flight-path - torn into tatters - the great undertaking - angel imprints in the snow - a perfectly good design - walls of indifference - suitable for the form.

I've been married – married twice. I've been single in between. I've lived for myself and lived for others at different times.

Been the child in a wonderful family. Been an adult in two more. Not a care in the world at times and at other times, weighted down with care.

So what do I find in the big fat book – with every wise man getting a chapter of weighty thought?

Very little, I would say, to get me through the day. Not worth the candle to light up a single page in the dark.

Then the two
took hold of the rope
at the same end.

This town is paradise to me. A child can play in the streets and fields. Grow up and go to school. One can go to church on Sunday. Every month a meeting at the lodge. The sun comes up over the tree-tops. It sets just over the river, past the bridge. There's nothing anywhere else that isn't available right here.

Once while digging neath the snow.

Just two lines – two minuscule lines, though the letters are tinged with gold – to use as a newspaper advertisement in the coming week:

Will you please let me go, Ma.
To McIntyres to buy a sofa.

The opening of gates and portals and doors.
A writer with a tooth-ache or a broken string.
A poet who writes poems that no one reads.

I think of tears as a futile attempt to quench a raging fire of immense pain.

Odysseus, he of the great adventure
To have a feast upon a trencher
Would pause a while to taste the delicious
Salad, which was quite nutritious

Are you aware there has to be an epic quest?
On what quest will your epic hero be engaged?
The single focus of the hero's every thought?

Angels have no need to write.

One – the chronicler of the past in dramas great.
And one – the chronicler of the present, a challenging feat.

What would religion and war be without bread and cheese?

Dance with a unicorn at daybreak. Dance with a unicorn at night. Keep
your distance, in the darkness, from the horn.

Clearing the land of walnut trees.
A field of potatoes attacked by potato bugs.
Allegiance to the flag and the Queen.

Puzzling out the structure of my epic poem.
If a block of cheese sets out on a voyage, and there must be something that
it is seeking, and it cannot be seeking itself – the block of cheese – and the hero
of the poem cannot be the block of cheese, then it follows that what the hero is
seeking must be some other prize than the block of cheese.

We are counting on Toronto. Toronto will put us over the top. The highest
mountain, the highest promontory, the highest hill. We need Toronto as we
need sustenance. More than water, air or food. We need a boost from the Toronto judges – a Toronto catapult to fling us up to the stars.
And I felt like shipwrecked on the strand.
Should it be billed as – 'The Biggest' – 'The Largest' – 'The Foremost in
Size'? For sure it is – for sure it is. The only thing wanting now is validation.
What is fact must be acknowledged. What is true must be affirmed. A certificate – a certificate of significance. Then a hammer and a nail and the nearest
tree.

Cooped up in a house of sorrow. Playing nurse-maid to his brother, Tom.
Tom spitting out his lungs drop by drop. Risking his own health for his brother.
Wondering whether he too was developing a cough.

"Goes on all the lodge-trips to the nearby towns."
"Writes a poem about each one."

Trelawny and I piling driftwood on the fire. Trelawny nursing the arm he burnt retrieving the still-beating heart. "I should have gone with him, Trelawny – queasiness or no. I could have raised the anchor and reefed the sails." 'The Double-loss of the Double-greatness of Shelley and McIntyre.' The day is cold. We shiver and scrounge the beach. We toss the gathered driftwood onto the bier.

What do you know - what do i do now - the sad account - applying my key - made of cloud - not a sign - the rarest gem - add to her nomens - carried wherever life takes us - regretted-alternative adventure.

So what's my philosophy, you ask. The one I didn't get from a book? The one I learned from the sweat of my brow and the skin of my nose?
The one I acquired from the rising of the sun? The one I acquired from the sun at noon? The one I acquired from being bone-tired at the end of the day?
The one from seeing the town burn down? The one from watching the river rise? The one from witnessing friends and loved-ones pass away?

They named the parts
that were at war.

Watching children playing in the snow on a winter morning. The sunlight making sparkles on the snow. They romp and play and throw a few snowballs. Then their mother calls them for lunch. They leave little angel-images in the field.
Glowing like pearls of great price.
Sitting and writing as the snow piles up on the window-sill. A chronicle of the life of our town:

When winter comes it brings no gloom,
But makes fresh pleasures spring and bloom,
For when the youth longs for a bride
He gives his girl a grand sleigh ride.

Lying in the gutters of the imagination. Lying in the cess-pools of despair. Dying for want of a crust of bread or a sugar-plum. His talent a loaf of mouldering bread on the shelves of the literary world. One more young poet not welcome anywhere.

Confusion in Toronto.

Surely things will be sorted out.

'Twas on a pleasant eve in May.
Just as the sun shed its last ray,
The bell it rang, citizens to warn,
For lo! A fire appears in barn.
The ancient barn near hotel stood,
The joining buildings all were wood;
This barn a relic of the past,
There farmers' horses were made fast.
Our once fair town is now in woe,
And we have had our Chicago;
But soon a nobler town will rise,
For Ingersoll's all enterprise.
For water far town need not seek
As there is river and the creek.
Just find the means it to apply
And then all fire must quickly die.

Have you recovered - was born to be - they go together - pick the pieces
up - it is cryptic - much more interesting - no one seems to know - this time,
though - all i will say about that - what was the point.

Well, the sun rises every morning. It climbs as high as it can in the sky. And
so should I.

The sun pauses in the heavens. It takes stock at the mid-point of the day.
And so should I.

The sun goes down every evening. Gives the best of himself each day.
Seems to me that I should always do the same.

Did you listen to what the other wise man said?

The horses pause as if in awe of the task that they have undertaken. A huge
banner hangs over the gates of the Toronto Exhibition. 'Come and See the
Largest Chunk of Cheese in the Whole Wide World!'
And in a voice of thunder as I sat at the table.
Validation! Validation! Validation! At times we hold the globe in our hand.
We hold it up to the sunlight. Through the window, a gentle breeze. The world
is a sphere of blank white paper. We dip our pen in the ink and make our mark.

There was the open-house for the new enterprise. The furniture-display
shop in the front. The woodworking-manufactory in the back. The whole town
came out to have a look. My son and I showed everyone around.

Such happiness is seldom seen,

A staircase made of cloud.
Violets blooming beneath the snow.
A flower without a root.

Happier far than king or queen;

Something that every person needs?
Something that every society wants?
The something that has been missing, so far, in their lives?

She helped him in the fields to reap,
And spun the wool from off the sheep,

I write little poems for all the surrounding communities. A bunch of us go to these places for lodge-meetings on the train. St. Thomas – London – Port Stanley. I write it during the meeting and read it out at the end. I make a copy for the local newspaper before I leave town.

If you don't believe this wondrous story.

"It is possible to consider that such revered poets as Keats, Shelley and Coleridge have attained such heights of perfection in their most exquisite poetry as to be admired as celestial beings, from afar, and yet, sadly, to be somehow unconnected with those of us with our feet in the mud, the mire and – may I say it? – the dung of life here, on the ground. Not so – we are bound to say – with our earth-bound poet – that man-of-the-commonest-concerns – James McIntyre."

Chapter 10
Toronto 3

The judging starts in an hour. A last-minute rumour sweeps the crowd. I can't believe that this is happening! This is history repeating itself! They brought us all the way here to tell us now! But what about the banner at the gate? That banner is the reason for the size of this crowd!

Bubbles that glitter ere they rise and break.

How could history be happening again? How could the stars be so amiss? What are the stumbling-blocks that plague the human course? To reach for the sun with the barest of hands! Surely a quest for the son of a god! To bring home the gold at the end of the rainbow! – the golden fleece! – the massive cheese! And then be greeted by empty streets and an absent crowd!

The river is different

A competition without a prize.
A man who is almost late for lunch.
An exception which is made in a particular case.

each time

Where did you meet your first wife?
Was it love at first sight or love delayed?
Do you remember the day that you proposed?

I sit here on the bench.

An evaporator for drying fruit.
A list of wars in Queen Victoria's reign.
Great pumpkins and huge ears of corn.

A thought will travel from the mind to the end of a finger. The thought will turn around and travel back again. The thought will talk to other thoughts.

Where have you been and what have you done? Then it will turn around and travel back again.

Would all but stoop to what they understand.

We lose ourselves and are found by others. We lose others and find them ourselves. Life is continually losing and finding and losing again.

There were thorns in the pathway. There were torrents in the creek. The bright light still shone on the mountain. The path in the valley was narrow and steep. Armour dented, sword bent, he forged ahead.

Farmers now cannot be beat
With their cheese and their wheat,
Though now their greatest care is
For to watch o'er their dairies.

"We got the greatest piece of cheese in the British Empire."
"And we got the poet who can put her into words."

A big black void! A big black void with fangs! Opening its jaws! The path would be its tongue! I am walking on that path!

Spent his life - both the same - make them whole - make a necklace - too big to fit - how vital this designation - albatross fell off - taken into the mind - a will and a single idea - the thing that i have thought.

What else am I working on, in the mean time? Well, I don't confine myself to epics, that's for sure. In fact '*The Mammoth Cheese*' will be the first epic that I shall have tried.

As you might expect, I often write about writers and writing. I have some poems about the English poets. And some poems about the Scottish writers as well.

I have poems about Canada and its people. Poems about Brock's Monument and of course, Niagara Falls. But these are merely what I would call 'hymns of the everyday'.

If they were
you and I would be different too.

Another emergency meeting – 'Emergency Meeting Number What'? Where is the list where I was keeping track? I flip the pages back through time but no note appears. It's in the notebook which I filled and filed away in my 'Reportage' drawer. Only the judges and those concerned. I press my case with the men at the door. Surely the public has a right to know! This concerns every man, woman and child in Ingersoll! All I have heard are speculative rumours!

Surely you want the truth to be told! I am the voice of the common populace! I insist that I hear the news and pass it on!

A half-blown flow'ret which cold blasts amate.

What is the news that is no news? What is the newspaper without a headline? What is the story that is printed as a blank page? What are the facts when there are no facts? What are the thoughts that are based on nothing – nothing at all?

There were thorns in the pathway. There were torrents in the creek. The bright light still shone on the mountain. The path in the valley was narrow and steep. Armour dented, sword bent, he forged ahead.

They carefully fill their mows
With provender for their cows,
And they thus enrich the soil
With much profit for their toil.

A failure to reach an agreement.
Watching the judges ply their trade.

O how I wish that two paths diverged! Then I would take the other path! The path that was not a big back void! The path that was not a tongue! The path that did not have two fangs!

The urgency is clear - wouldn't want to lose - the arbiter of thought - the grand unveiling - too off-guard - swallowed a compass - glue that failed to hold - a drop of rain - a very fundamental distinction - both rocks and shoals.

Was Homer a god – or simply a man? Was Virgil a human being? Was Milton not a regular person, like you or me?

Who wrote these wonderful epics? Each was a boy, when he started out, with a massive dream. I have a pen, I have plenty of paper and gallons of ink.

My dream is to be the chronicler of this great epic journey. The humble chronicler, I need not add, and I'm sure you'll agree. The glory will be all to the cheese – none to me.

It was amazing
how easily the rope
was made to move.

Something was nipping at his toes. What was it? He had swum in these waters before. He had sat on the bank and listened to stories galore. He hadn't paid much attention to what had been said.

The very knowledge that he lived in vain.

I am a widower. I lost my wife. It can seem like yesterday. It can seem like years.

Thoughts that are deeper than our thoughts.
An easy-chair that causes the back to ache.
Exploring the wreckage of a town.

The motto 'Union is Strength'
Is carried out at length
In the most compact array
At every cheese factory.

I think of the beating of my heart as two clocks ticking in the same room.

When sprinkled with oregano and olive oil.
Product of his native soil.
Aged in barrels filled with brine.
Served along with a favourite wine.

Where did you live when you first got married?
Is it true that you built a house?
And you planned the house together, I assume?

Angels communicate among themselves without words.

I write – I trust, the very gods to please –
Of the epic voyage of the Mammoth Cheese.

He would plumb the poetic heights.

Plant in the morning and the yield will be heavy. Plant in the evening and the yield will be light. The scythe is at its sharpest at break of day.

The editor of a local newspaper.
Taking tea at the Ladies' Aid.
An old church in a maple grove.

Oh Mr. Harris always knows just what to do.
Mr. Harris will always come up with something new.

A scrum of Ingersollians. Outside the exhibition hall. The manufacturers speak to the crowd. No category for our splendid enterprise – no acknowledgment of our accomplishment – no recognition of our great deed – no prize for what they admit is excessive size. Only the taste of a little piece will the judges see. I catch a glimpse of Mr. Harris through the half-open door.

As is a landscape to a blind man's eye.

Not open to the world? – not open to the world? What kind of logic is 'not open to the world'? Only open to Ontario? – only Ontarians allowed to compete? That is why the judges will award no world-level prize? But it's the biggest cheese in the world! Their own banner proclaims the fact! How could they put that banner up and not give a prize?

There were thorns in the pathway. There were torrents in the creek. The bright light still shone on the mountain. The path in the valley was narrow and steep. Armour dented, sword bent, he forged ahead.

You''ll see without going as far as
There is one kept by Harris,
The factory of Ingersoll,
Just out at the first toll.

"Always ready to stop and chat."
"Always a handshake and a smile."

Is it possible that I am asleep? That this void is merely a dream? That there is no black void with fangs! Oh I hope that it is a dream! Do dreams have any connection to life at all?

Into another stream - certainly happen for sure - everything would be all right - opening the doors - a central idea - humans try to understand - ends of the earth - philosophical woe - glues of different kinds - a mental holiday.

The great epic, I know, will be a certainty. A certainty, for sure, I know it will be. And the poem of this great event will write itself.

All I have to do is follow the progress of the adventure. The story will be the story of the Mammoth Cheese. I'll simply take the events and turn them into rhyme.

The cheese is fact – an enormous fact. Its future course is as predictable as the rising and the setting of the sun. All I have to do is tag along and write.

They made adjustments
and sent the patient on his way.

Back home there were snapping turtles. They would nip at a swimmer's toes. Swimmers would swim like no one's business. Practically fly right up on the bank. Don't want a snapping turtle taking ahold of your toe.

A hope beyond the shadow of a dream.

Go back to Scotland some future day. See some of the places I didn't get to see. Who would be there, I wonder, to talk to about those who are gone.

There were thorns in the pathway. There were torrents in the creek. The bright light still shone on the mountain. The path in the valley was narrow and steep. Armour dented, sword bent, he forged ahead.

All those who quality do prize
Must study colour, taste and size,
And keep their dishes clean and sweet
And all things round their factories neat;
For dairymen insist that these
Are all important points in cheese.

Disappointment in Toronto.
A somber train ride home.

Heard melodies are sweet, but those unheard
Are sweeter; therefore, ye soft pipes, play on;
Not to the sensual ear, but, more endear'd,
Pipe to the spirit ditties of no tone:
Fair youth, beneath the trees, thou canst not leave
Thy song, nor ever can those trees be bare;
Bold Lover, never, never canst thou kiss
Though winning near the goal—yet, do not grieve;
She cannot fade, though thou hast not thy bliss,
For ever wilt thou love, and she be fair!

A god would please - old, old story - wait for the letters to settle - an all-night guard - than are dreamt of - times we spent together - lived significant episodes - fit into all this - all I have to say - a valid term.

But the question, as I recall, was about my secondary projects. The poems that I write, as it were, on the side. The poems of limited potential for renown.

Well, I have one poem of which I am pleasantly pleased. A poem about a couple. A man and woman who were what we call 'pioneers'.

Two people who made a life for themselves out of what little they originally had. They carved a home out of the wilderness, near Ingersoll. They're names are John and Jane Roe.

I didn't have to, said one wise man,
as I could tell
by what many people told me
that the shallow fool
had stolen my best ideas.

A somber train-ride home to Ingersoll. All are tired from their excitement at the fair. The manufacturers puff their cigars at the front of the railway car. A flask is passed around from hand to hand. I ask to sit among them but I am refused. They will make their public statement when the time is right. There is very little talk. Each is absorbed in his own little world. I see the back of Mr. Harris's head but not his eyes.

And I blessed them unaware.

I rack my brain to consider the facts. Here is a lesson, sure enough. There is the cheese – there is the prize. I see that he who controls the cheese controls nothing at all. I see that he who controls the prize controls the world. Pin a blue ribbon on this or that – confer value on what you prefer or hold it back. Make here a king or a duke or maybe an earl – make there a miserable peasant or a slave. Turn a blind eye to the biggest mountain of cheese in the world.

Each side of river hath its work
Devoted to the cure of pork,
For dairymen find it doth pay
To fatten pigs upon the whey;
For there is money raising grease
As well as in the making cheese.

I stay away from the shop at times. Attendance at the lodge-meetings – the reporting of special events in town – the writing of poems as I sit by the river on a bench. I'm the boss so I don't always have to be there. I can still see the traces of blood on the manufactory floor. We sanded it, but the thought remains to this day.

All they required they had for both,

Judges who are wearing blind-folds.
Ideas smouldering inside the head.
A walking-stick which is stuck in the mud.

Of her own weaving of good cloth,

How many years were you married, in all?
What was the cause of your wife's demise?
What did you say to your son when you told him his mother had died?

And she was a good tailoress,
Did make his coat and her own dress;

But here there were different stories. Every once in a while there were mermaids. They would tickle a swimmer's toes. How did the stories go after that? He should have listened as the people on the bank had talked.

As mine-lamps enkindle a hidden gem.

The water flows beneath the bridge. You could look straight down at the water between the planks when it was wood. I close my eyes and the water moves backward from whence it came.

Chapter 11
Ingersoll 5

There is quiet in the town. The postman brings the mail. The children go to school. The barber cuts the hair. The bill collector raps sharply on the door. The old fellow has his nap in the easy-chair.

They circle closer around him.

There is tension in the town. What we think and never say – what we say and never think. We have cast ourselves on the waters. We are many leagues from shore. Why is the vessel not moving forward? Is there a leak in the boat or have we run aground?

Sometimes

Two journalists touring a town.
A dot on the map of the globe.
A question which generates a detailed response.

the river is swollen

Have you considered your own qualifications?
To write yourself an epic poem?
What you are as a writer and as a man?

with all the recent spring rains.

A monument to a fallen hero.
A husband who is always at his lodge.
A visit by the Prince of Wales.

I enjoy reading my poems. I read them in public whenever I can. Whenever I am asked at a special event. I compose them in my spare time. People give me ideas sometimes. They suggest who I should turn their stories into rhyme.

Imagination's grandest theme.

A poem is being a mirror and not being you. Just for a moment, you are standing outside of yourself. A poem is you being the mirror and the mirror being you. You no longer see the mirror – the mirror sees you. A poem is you changing places with yourself.

Scandal piled on scandal. Reviled as a breaker of social taboos. A failed marriage and many affairs. Mounting debts and mounting scandal. Shaking the cloying dust of England from his feet.

"He left the church and then came back."
"Had a few things to figure out is all it was."

A room by the Spanish Steps. Severn needs a break and I inform him that I would be glad to watch the young poet as he sleeps. Severn takes exception, but I shoo him away. What though I expose myself to consumption? – what of that? "An honour," I say to Severn. "An honour it would be – to have caught the consumptive malady from the lungs of John Keats."

As to whether I won - every subject was stained - there was no damage - an unbroken girdle - your hopes and your dreams - every drop in the ocean - awakening to the possibilities - make the trek - all losses are restor'd - my fingerprints.

Now – let me ask a simple question. Let me turn the tables on you. Let me ask a blunt question and let you squirm.

Why the intense personal interest? Why not content yourself with questions about my verse? Why the concern with what I am in my daily life?

Why do you tell me about yourself? Your interests and your dreams? Why insist that all your linen be aired on the line?

Two birds
shared a nest.

A dim light in the window of the factory. Mr. Harris is burning the midnight oil. A lantern swings in the darkness. Not to be disturbed says the night-watch-man at the gate. Alone he sits – Mr. Harris – I can testify to that. Alone in his office all night. Alone he sits and burns the midnight oil.

And witches did play many a trick.

Grim days for Mr. Harris – the admiral of the fleet. Oh such a simple plan. Such a simple, simple plan. Show the cheese at many gatherings. At the exhibitions and fairs. Let a groundswell grow throughout the land. A cheer so loud that it reaches to Britain – to Paris and beyond. The largest cheese in the whole wide world! Stand in the bow as you cross the Atlantic. Wave the certificate as you sail across the sea.

A dark night in an old castle. Candles flickering as they talked. Each agreed to write a story. Each would tell a frightening tale. The candles flickered though the room was tightly locked.

The news from Toronto.
Taking stock in Ingersoll.

John Keats furrows his brow. I lift his head – cradled in my arms – and he sips from the glass that I proffer. "Here lies one whose name was writ in water", he sighs, and sinks back, exhausted, on the pillow. "Nay, John", I say, "You shall be among the English poets after your death."

The wickets are closed - see nothing detrimental - refuses to be interviewed - perused the great philosophers - sense of equitable terms - to know and to see - i think of you - the night-mare need - giving something back - deliberately avoided.

I asked to hear about your town. About the activities here-abouts. About the landscape and the festivals and things.

That is what I write about. I write of the life of the community. I write about the people as public people, not private lives.

That is what I expect from you. Simply what is your function – what is your role. Not your hopes and dreams and failures. Not the talons that are tearing apart your soul.

The moon influences
the tides on earth.

Keats and Shelley and all these poets have a lot to say. They always manage to find the appropriate rhymes. If their poems didn't rhyme, I don't know whether I'd be so interested. I'd choose rhyming thoughts over not-rhyming thoughts any day.

Swept through the dark passage 'neath the road.

Canada – my Canada. I celebrate your attributes – as the Ancient Greeks used to do – in poetic song:

We'll tell a tale, it shall be brief.
It is a tale of Maple Leaf,
From noble Olive Branch it sprung,
And its good deeds shall yet be sung.

A sky with two suns.
An iron-clad agreement about words.

A hero washing up on a shore.

I think of our two hearts as two pails on a cloudy day waiting for rain.

The god of cheese is Aristaios.
He a son was of Apollo's.
Working together they
Would work their magic with curds and whey.

What in your life makes you heroic?
What in your life is an epic quest?
What in your life, would you say, is a journey of danger and risk?

Angels communicate at deeper levels of thought than humans tend to do.

We intend to ship the enormous fromage across the ocean
To the land we all call England, or sometimes Britain.

Pull the roots up out of his soul.

The corn will arrange itself in rows. The cucumbers will sprawl all over the garden. Each has a destiny that only a seed can know.

Leaves sprouting on the trees in the spring.
Trees of beach and maple and elm.
Concentrating the essence of a tale.

Oh Mr. Harris is a man of great resolve.
There is no challenge that Mr. Harris cannot solve.

Trying to tend to the task at hand. Sell the goods and pay the bills. Stand on the sidewalk once in a while and say hello. Try to ignore the rumours sweeping up and down the street.
Which doth suffer this great wrong.
The plug should be pulled! The plug should definitely be pulled! I say the plug should be pulled and that is that! No – the plug should not be pulled! The plug should definitely not be pulled! Ingersollians only move forward – Ingersollians do not cut and run! I say it's Hamilton next and then we go overseas!

What is the price of one's humanity? What is the choice that must be made? To nurse one's brother on his sickbed? To stay alive for one's writing and one's love? Why does life sometimes make us make choices like this?

"He can rhyme like nobody's business."

"He's a master at handling words."

His furrowed brow clears and he whispers through smiling lips, "Yes, James, I am sure that you are right in your conjecture. We shall both of us be remembered. I am sure that, in future, one will not say the word 'Keats' without saying "Keats and McIntyre' and one will not say 'McIntyre' without saying 'McIntyre and Keats'. Two comets, clog-dancing, arm-in-arm, in the poetic sky." He closes his eyes and is able, at last, to sleep.

One of these might suit - when occasion serves - humans come close - often wondered - something different to everyone - pounce upon the story - have the same meaning - haul was disappointing - another person's voice - all those medals.

Is Homer's name found in the *Iliad*? Is Shakespeare's name found in the plays? Does the death of a wife or son ever appear?

Their hopes and their dreams when they were young? Their disappointments in middle age? The tears they cried when their plans went up in smoke?

They write of sailors and soldiers and kings. They write of ships and rocks and storms. They write of battles and journeys and gods who manipulate things.

The clock
had an impish sense of humour.

We used to skate on the creek below the bridge. A little too old for it now. Freeze-up comes in November or late-October. Skate all winter until break-up comes in March. Leave a log out on the rink to test the ice. Now, I content myself with watching from the bridge.

And of his power gives ample proof.

Recalling a visit that my wife and I made to Niagara Falls. At times like these, the poems seem to write themselves. Actually – both wives – my second wife and my first – but not of course, at the same time.

Thus the world's great wonder
Reverberates like peals of thunder.
Enshrined with mist and beauteous glow
Of varied tints of the rainbow.

He couldn't write in his own voice. He couldn't write in his own time. Voices spoke to him from a distance. Voices guided the pen in his hand. Voices told him anciently to write and to anciently spell.

Pressing ahead on the journey.
Things will be different from now on.

Come listen, while we sound the lyre,
To announce that McIntyre
Is back again to his old block,
And he has got a splendid stock.
He also hath a strong desire
To see old friends, and new acquire;
His furniture is cheap and good,
In every style and kind of wood.
But none in health need e'er despair,
If they buy from him an easy chair.
When you his Warehouse then do seek,
'Tis where the brick bridge spans the creek.

One can be human - make the best of this - the bottom of the sea - a shadow looms ahead - mixes with the blood - the basic needs - no need to talk - comin' along pretty good - take care of itself - living in half a house.

The great writers never write about themselves. I don't expect to talk about me when I talk to you. I don't expect to listen to your personal agonies and despairs.

Did Shakespeare have a tooth-ache when he was writing about King Lear? Did Homer break a string on his lyre when he was singing of the battle of Troy? Why did neither write his memoirs and leave them behind?

So – no more personal questions, please. I'll ask no personal questions of you. Great literature is not a mail-bag stuffed with the gossip of the day.

He broke into the safe at the bank.
He put all the money in a sack.

An interview with Mr. Harris – the admiral of the fleet. A request for an assessment of the quest. I see the man – I hear him speak. But when is an interview not an interview?

And while engaged in scenes like these.

Now is not the time, Mr. McIntyre, for an interview. Though I respect your role as scribe of this event. I have Toronto-poison strangling my veins. Now is definitely not the time for an interview. The words that I am feeling should definitely not be rendered into print.

It was a problem with the lathe. It was a lathe of my design. All the belts seemed to be in their proper places. It had worked well for a month at least. Just the right tension in the pulleys and the belts. It seemed – at the time – a perfectly good design. Until the day I heard the commotion from the back of the shop.

The golden butter that she made

A man who designs his own house.
A composer who cannot remember a tune.
A new bridge made of brick.

Was of the very finest grade,

What have been your life's epic ecstasies?
What have been your life's epic agonies?
What events have cast your life on an epic scale?

Each grace and virtue she possess'd,
Where'er she was, that spot was blessed,

People tell me that I should run for Mayor. Since I'm always singing the praises of the town. I say I don't want the cares of office. I have enough cares of my own. People purr at me and growl when they see the Mayor.

Gazing on mighty orbs of fire.

"There is an underground grapevine in the poetic community and through that method of concept-communication news travels furiously and fast. Word has it that the poem-in-development of the noted poet, James McIntyre – dubbed '*The Mammoth Cheese*' – will, when it is completed, hit the poetic world with the force of a tropical storm."

Chapter 12
Hamilton 1

At the station, in the morning, bound for Hamilton. The cheese-box slides into place once again. The workmen shut and seal the door. All aboard who are going aboard. The whistle sounds – the engine chugs – we are under way.

He played an ancient ditty long since mute.

A smaller crowd on board than for the earlier excursions. Some dropped off after Saratoga – been neglecting things at home. Some dropped off after Toronto – got to get back to the daily routine. Some vow to stay with the Mammoth Cheese through thick and thin.

Sometimes

A rift on the ocean floor.
A town returning to normal.
The secret of turning milk into cheese.

I brush off the snow

How did you feel the day that your son was born?
Was it a difficult birth for your wife?
Was he more like your wife, do you think, or like you?

before I sit down.

An axe hewing a maple bough.
Clouds of snow during a storm.
Tea and cakes and pumpkin pies.

Does the leaf of a tree talk to the root? Does the root of a tree talk to the leaf? If they do talk to each other what do they say? Does each tell all that he knows? Or are there secrets that are kept and never shared?

The wise want love and those who love want wisdom.

Write the words of your innermost longings. Write the words of your innermost soul. I am the only one you can write this to in the world.

A dark night in an old castle. Candles flickering as they talked. Each agreed to write a story. Each would tell a frightening tale. The candles flickered though the room was tightly locked.

"That's always the way with Trawna."
"They won't let nobody get ahead."

I am walking along on the edge of a cliff! The waves crash on the rocks below! The sun is shining from above! The grass is green in the fields! The wind is blowing with leather lungs!

Just beneath the surface - bricks mortared into a wall - weighted down with care - seem a little odd - in an aside - a bigger uniform - settle down into place - my day away - back to the everyday - a language that hides the life.

So what kind of writer am I? Well, that is a very interesting question. I've certainly noticed that there are different kinds of writers.

There is the writer who is in control of the life, but not in control of the writing. And there is the writer who is in control of the writing, but not in control of the life. And you are asking, I assume, what kind of writer am I.

But, of course, if you think about it, it's a little bit more complicated than that. There's the writer, we would hope, who is in control of both the writing and the life. And there is the writer, alas, who is not in control of the writing or the life.

One was a winter bird;
one was a summer bird.

We chug along on the Hamilton leg of our quest. The front of the railway car is wreathed in gloom. Cigar-smoke fills the air – loud clearing of throats and much spitting at the spittoons. Mr. Harris keeps himself busy with pencil and pad.

With what I most enjoy contented least.

The factory owners do not talk among themselves. No longer the optimistic chatter on the way to Saratoga. No longer the confident discussion of odds on the way to Toronto. These are the captains of the enterprise. The saga limps along. Plenty of thoughts, perhaps, that no one wishes to share.

Woes in Italy. Woes back home. Writing poems. Writing pamphlets. When will injustice stumble and fall upon its sword?

Arriving in Hamilton.
A trainload of Ingersollians.

What is the meaning of a cliff? Why am I walking along the edge? What is the meaning of green grass? What is the meaning of waves and rocks? Is the wind blowing on-land or blowing off-shore?

I stay behind - empty into the ocean - ain't no judge - poems that no one reads - arms around the world - an all-night guard - left around the bend - didn't bother to open - extension of the mind - wounded by a metaphor.

So what of Shakespeare, Shelley, Keats, Wordsworth, Byron? How do we take these writers and place them on a grid? There would be two grids, I imagine – one for the writing and one for the life.
Or maybe four grids? Or could it be six? Or would it be eight?
Successful writing and successful life – successful writing and not-successful life – not-successful writing and successful life – not-successful writing and not-successful life.

I'm pleased to know that
said the man in the moon.

A honey bee was telling a story. The young bees listened as the elder talked. They hovered in a circle as he explained. It was the secret of the ages. They were learning to make honey for the hive.
By our own spirits are we deified.
Just the three of us. Walking along. Not going anywhere in particular. A pleasant day.

Two men shifting a charred timber.
A concert down at the local schoolhouse.
A river with a dark forest on either side.

I think of memories as a doctor who is letting blood.

Other gods would envious be.
Gods of wine and other eats
Would wonder at the recipes
Made from this ambrosial cheese.

What were the games your son played in the summers?
What were the winter activities the whole family enjoyed?
What did you ask him every night as you put him to bed?

Angels think and other angels know what they mean.

Perhaps the Queen could be enticed to grant a wish.
After she has tasted the cheese in a dish

Make great literature out of the rib-bone of his life.

One horse ran east. One horse ran west. They planned to meet on the other side. In the end, only one horse came back home.

Working all day at a logging bee.
The beauty and the wonder of Niagara Falls.
A bridge over a river.

Puzzling out the structure of my epic poem.
If a block of cheese sets out on a voyage, and there must be something that it is seeking, and it cannot be seeking itself – the block of cheese – and the hero of the poem cannot be the block of cheese, and what the hero is seeking must be some other prize than the block of cheese, then it follows that what the hero is seeking must be an indication of validation from a wise and trusted source.

Idle chatter among the Ingersoll crowd in the back of the railway car. I can't wait to get to England. I have a passel of relatives there. It's the centre of the Empire – the eyes of all the world. I'm the boy who left with nothing. I'll be strutting when I return. I'll be basking in the glow of the Ingersoll Cheese.
Let our frail thoughts dally with false surmise.
What's the matter with those Americans? What's the problem with Toronto? We put them both in the shade. They had to cheat to keep feeling superior. Had to put the blinders on. Couldn't admit that they'd been bested. We're the only town to have a massive cheese.

Coughing up blood on the handkerchief. Coughing up blood on the written page. Struck by the hooves of galloping consumption. Perhaps a winter in a warmer clime. Fanny promised to be waiting when he returned.

"Writes about everything that happens."
"Born to write – like all them great writers in the past."

I am walking along the edge of a cliff! The grass grows greener in the field! The waves crash louder on the rocks! Is the wind on-shore or off-shore? The leather lungs are blowing a stronger and stronger wind!

A man who never deviates - never been here before - find a suitable rhyme
- what have i learned - keep your distance - the times we had - an unbroken

girdle - followed the progress - a welcome draught - he sat and watched.

So what of Chaucer – the life and the poems? What of Homer – the life and the epics? What of Milton – the life and the writing of *Paradise Lost*?

What of Blake, Wordsworth, Coleridge? What of Byron, Shelley and Keats? What kind of writer would we take these authors to be?

And what of Shakespeare – the ultimate author? Of the great plays there can be no doubt. But there's a paucity of information to fit on the grid.

Once in a while
the clock would change the time.

He was amazed that he could listen. That a human could understand. He was learning the honey-bee secret. Every nuance of every buzz. How to make the golden honey for the hive.

The fierce dispute between damnation and impassioned clay.

My mother stoking the fire. My father coming in from the barn. Wiping the frost off the glass with the sleeve of my shirt.

He wrote a series of ancient poems. Wrote in the jargon of earlier days. Pretended that he was a medieval poet. Presented his counterfeit scripts to the world. Many an expert was taken in and the poet was praised.

Ready for the big adventure.
Pencil, paper and expertise.

I met a traveller from an antique land
Who said: Two vast and trunkless legs of stone
Stand in the desert.... Near them, on the sand,
Half sunk, a shattered visage lies, whose frown,
And wrinkled lip, and sneer of cold command,
Tell that its sculptor well those passions read
Which yet survive, stamped on these lifeless things,
The hand that mocked them, and the heart that fed:
And on the pedestal these words appear:
'My name is Ozymandias, king of kings:
Look on my works, ye Mighty, and despair!'
Nothing beside remains. Round the decay
Of that colossal wreck, boundless and bare
The lone and level sands stretch far away.

A narrow opening - the spectacular unveiling - defends the battlements - abrasive grit - flagpole that had fallen - perused the great philosophers - deeper than our dreams - the mixing is thoroughly accomplished - have anything to say - a door that is barred.

And what about me, I believe you are asking. Where do I put myself on such a grid? How do I judge myself – as a writer – as a self?

The one – I would say – is out of my hands. Friends and family can judge me while I exist in this vale of tears. Ultimately it is between myself and God.

Too early to tell, I would have to say, for the other. My greatest work still lies gloriously ahead. The fate of my epic poem will determine that toss of the dice.

He went home and put the money in a monogrammed pillow-case.
Next day, he took his pillow-case to the bank.

The sun is shining through the window. The train clicks over the rails. Miles go by as we cross the country-side. Mr. Harris sits and figures. Mr. Harris doesn't talk. Mr. Harris moves the pencil across the page. Mr. Harris doesn't know I am staring at him.

A thousand fleets sweep over thee in vain.

The same suit – the same hat. The same brand of expensive cigar. The same stick-pin in the very same cravat. Mr. Harris looks the same as when we started out on this quest, but is he the same man who created the Mammoth Cheese?

It concerned my only son. The blood was pumping from his stomach. He was lying on the floor and the belt was flapping as the lathe went round and round. It was an agony of pain. We carried him across the street to the doctor. The blood is on that floor to this very day.

And though they did not have stove then,

Cold water flowing from a fountain.
A room in the back of a dry-goods store.
A Jason without the Golden Fleece.

Neither did they own an oven;

How long had your son been working in the furniture-factory?
Was he eager to take over the business someday?
How old was your son when the accident occurred?

She filled large pot with well knead dough
And baked fine bread 'mong embers glow;

The elder bee finished his story. The novice bees flew off on their rounds. They would soon be making honey for the hive. As he watched his heart was breaking. He knew that he could never be a bee.

On the shore of the wide world I stand alone.

Eyes closed as I sit on the bench. The sunlight comes right through my eyelids and finds my thoughts and illuminates my mind.

Chapter 13
Hamilton 2

Not an exhibition at all. Just a day of races at the track. We attracted more attention as we made our way from the train station, with our massive box of cheese, than waiting here, at the track, for the races to start.

In it's own place 'tis very good.

Not a banner outside the gates. Not a sign as we move inside. I tell them I'm 'press' at the box-office window, but they make me pay. No one seems to know when the cheese-judging will start.

I sit and write

Talking of how to make honey for the hive.
A rumour that sweeps a crowd.
Pulling the roots up out of one's soul.

or I polish

Will there be a descent into the underworld in your epic poem?
What do you know about a descent into Hell?
What in your life has prepared you to write such an episode?

one of my poems.

A horse race in winter on the ice.
The ringing of merry sleigh bells.
Driftwood on the sands of a lake.

Cheddar cheese is my favourite cheese. There are other kinds, I know. I try other flavours from time to time. I always go back to cheddar. It seems to have the flavour that is right for me. In poetry I prefer the rhyming couplet.

And enshrined jewels in casket.

A poem weeps when it sits alone on a shelf. A poem is only happy when it is being read. A poem is like a slice of a vegetable or a piece of fruit. It does no good at all unless it is consumed. Unless it is taken into the mind – as fruit or vegetables are taken into the body – and digested – one can say that a poem is not a fruitful poem at all.

Bored with his life. Bored with his thoughts. Bored with the people that he knew. Hearing the ancient call to battle. Seeing the flag of freedom fly.

"It'll be great when we get to England."
"We'll all go to Buckingham Palace and shake hands with the Queen."

I rush to the rooms of Beethoven. I clutch a note in my hand. It is cryptic but the urgency is clear. Is the great one on his death-bed? 'My life is in your hands! Only you can save me! Pray – make haste and come to my side! If you fail me, the consequences shall be dire!'

I guarantee - take the temperature - think of what happened - the still-beating heart - planned to meet - pounce upon the story - we never awake - ever exchanged a word - brambles and thorns - consider yourself to be.

What demons did Homer face in the Hades of his imagination? To what underworld did he descend as he rode the cage to the bottom of the shaft? Who were the people who pointed their fingers with blazing eyes?

Byron lying in a fever at Missolonghi? What spirits was he seeing in his swampy underworld? Poking at him with the rusty blade of his personal pride?

Shelley bracing himself against the gunwale during the storm? What descent into fire and brimstone was threatened by the waves? What spirit – covered in seaweed – called to him from the depths of the Serpentine?

Keats tossing and turning on his sweat-soaked pillow? Chatterton ascending to the attic while descending, darkly, to the deepest depths inside?

To what Hell could I descend? To what after-world could I plunge down? What Hades is waiting to confront me when I die?

Whose divine buttock have I singed with a hot poker as I cleaned the clinkers from the Olympian grate? Whose solemn speech did I interrupt as I sneezed with hay-fever during an enclave of the gods? What sacred candle have I lit, inadvertently, whose wick-of-life was not meant to be my own?

I – a hummingbird with tired wings as I cling, exhausted, to a tiny twig on the lowest level of the heavenly tree? I – an ant whose belly drags in the dust as I crawl, penitently, on the thorns of sacred groves? What terrors can I expect as I am launched at the River Styx, arms folded, in a pine-box of my own design?

The winter bird was always too hot;
the summer bird was always too cold.

The horses race around the course. Not a word about us has been said. Too big to fit under the tunnel of the grandstand. The massive cheese sits in the stable-yard outside. The afternoon drags on. Most of the Ingersollians find themselves drifting inside. I sense an article as I move among the crowd.

Torrent onward rushes frantic.

I ain't never been to a race track. I ain't never bet before. I just had to give 'er a try. You just size up the horse and put your money down. Well, I don't know nothin' 'bout horses. I just go by the length of the legs. Now my wallet's just about empty. Well, I ain't no judge of horses, I can tell you that.

A relief from troubles. A break from philosophical woe. Sailing on a boat in the bay of Lerici. Taken by surprise by a sudden storm. Reef the sail and turn the prow into the waves.

The Mammoth Cheese in all its glory.
Hamilton and Ingersoll.

Beethoven lies in bed! There is agony on his brow! "I've lost my notes, James! – I've lost my memory! That time! – that time I hummed that tune! You were there – you said you liked it! And the poem to set it to?" He sinks back onto the pillow! My friend is clearly bereft! "If you cannot remember, I don't know what I shall do!"

Assessment of the journey - the single focus - o'erwhelmed in snow - have you considered - rib-bone of his life - everything beneath the sun - its immensity of presence - the bottom of the sea - years of perfecting - failed to defend the castle.

Despair has not been my forté. I do not wallow in self-regret. What are the soles – what is the bottom – of my concerns?

Is life a roadmap with the corner torn off? Is life a treasure map with no x? Is life a lamp with a missing wick? Is life an ocean with no bottom and no sides?

King Lear on the heath? Oedipus at Colonus? Prometheus chained to the rock? Is greatness a tantrum at broken toys on the nursery floor?

Take the heart from out the chest? Take the brain from out the skull? Take the knife and peel the covers from the eyes? Take the ears from off the head and thou shalt hear?

Dark without the sun. Dark without the moon. Dark with not a star in the sky.

Find the crevice on the surface of your mind. Take the spade and lift the sod and set it aside. Dig a hole the size of a grave as deep as you can.

Place a ladder in the hole and begin to descend. Take a lantern as a shield against the dark. I will wait beside the hole for your return.

The moon is made
of green cheese.

A rhyming couplet is a marvelous entity. It lends dull thought a luminous glow. There must be thousands of rhymes in the English language. I've used perhaps hundreds of rhymes myself. 'Cows- espouse' – 'cheese-disease' – 'her majesty-tragedy'. 'Asininity-sublimity' – 'irrelevant-intelligent' – 'tangential-central.' For every word one can find a suitable rhyme.

Until fair vision hove in sight.

The advertisements flow from my pen as the waters plunge from the heights of Niagara Falls. Full flood – full force – full bloom:

The people all say, and declare it's true,
The best furniture is made with McIntyre's glue.

A king who attacks and defends the battlements.
Two poets shoring up a sheepfold.
An ancient Bible with pictures.

I think of what happened to us as furniture-glue that failed to hold.

Apollo and his son would employ
For the other gods to enjoy
Manouri, Metsovone, Kasseri
Mizithra, Ladotyri, and Kefalotyri.

Will the hero be forced to confront his past?
Meet the people with whom he has lived significant episodes of his life?
Will he struggle to come to some sense of equitable terms?

Angel-imagery is a language that humans can barely understand.

And proclaimed it the most delicious cheese of all,
Her Majesty would pose beside the cheese from Ingersoll.

The blood from his head and heart would fill the page with ink.

The water is buoying you up on its surface. The water is taking you under its wing. The water is altering you and sending you down as rain.

Oxen drawing logs into a pile.
A mill grinding flour and oatmeal.
A group of men curling on the ice.

Oh Mr. Harris is the champion of all the world.
A sailing ship with all his banners brightly unfurled.

Hamilton is an interesting city. The bulk of it lies below an escarpment. Hamiltonians call this escarpment 'Hamilton Mountain' in solemn terms.

Triumphing with glorious voice.

You can call almost anything by any name. The question then is: who is speaking the words? If I say the words 'the mammoth cheese' does that phrase have the same meaning as when the very same phrase is spoken by Queen Victoria, the Empress of all the World, as she sits, between bites of Ingersoll cheese, on her Imperial Throne?

Would his name be writ in water? Would lasting fame be snuffed out? Would his pages be un-cut? Would his books gather dust? Would all the sedge be withered from his lake?

"Wonder why he don't publish a book."
"Oh he's going to – just as soon as he has enough poems."

"Yes, of course I remember, Ludwig." I hum the tune and a smile breaks forth on that agonized brow. "And the poem? – which was that? – do you, perchance, remember, James?" "Why Ludwig, it was Schiller's *'Ode to Joy'*!" "Oh, now I can finish my symphony! – I'm calling it my Ninth! Is there any way I can thank you? – perhaps I could name it after you!" "No need, Ludwig" – I whisper, as I fluff his pillow up – "no need at all."

On barren heath - a neglected well - more things in your philosophy - nothing moved - secret of the ages - can never mean a thing - weighted down with care - half in the light - every tick of his watch - the depths of thought.

Come on, now – you can't be serious – now why would I want to play a silly game? Exactly what do you want me to do? 'Look in your eyes and guess as much as I possibly can'?

Are you offering a prize? How do I figure out my score? Why don't you just tell me what you want me to know?

Well – I do have an idle hour. They tell me that nothing will happen for a while. So – I'll indulge your whim to pass away the time.

Now – let's see – you're obviously about ten years younger than me. Much like me in stature and size. The colour of hair and that wrinkle when you frown.

Starting out in your profession. Much like me when I was your age. I began, though, in an entirely different trade.

A little past the first bloom of youth. Settled into a life-routine. But young enough to retain your hopes and your dreams.

The man who owned the clock
did not have an impish sense of humour.

I've written articles on the making of the cheese. Very similar, I would say, to making a poem. Get an idea, make a plan, execute. If things go sour, you can always try again.

And on the waters it doth float.

A few lines on Doctor Gardner, who has faithfully served this town for many years:

Gardner told a sad tale of woe.
How he was oft o'erwhelmed in snow;
But was he frightened? No! No!! No!!!
He onward cheerfully did go.

His deception did not deceive. Not for ever and not for long. But was the young poet actually guilty of a fictional deception? Perhaps, in his imagination, the poet had lived in those early times. There are more things in your philosophy than are dreamt of out of your star, as Hamlet, himself, has often been heard to say.

Confusion in Hamilton.
An attempt to sort things out.

The farmers are in cheerful mood,
For harvest it hath all been good;
And all the grain was sown this spring
An abundant yield will bring.
And you can scarcely stow away
The yield of barley, oats and hay;
Such pasture it is seldom seen,
E'n now it is so fresh and green.
This beauteous colour nature decks
While it insures you large milk cheques,
And certes you've much cause to praise
For hogs and cattle that you raise.

World-encompassing experience - leave it exposed - nowhere in sight - saga limps along - half-buried in the sand - poems that no one reads - always a future - tracks in the mud - a torrent of full force - thoughts stick in my mind.

Old enough to be married, of course. I was younger than you are now. So – this is where I will start the guessing game.

Married, I would say. Married and happy, I would guess. Not every marriage produces the bloom that I see in you.

Children? You must like children. I guess for you a young son – a beautiful, cheerful, playful little boy.

In your profession – some discontent. The ladder is high – you are eager to climb. In your personal life, a shadow looms ahead.

What? – the game is over, my young friend? I pause without reply. Well then, some answers if you please – I am curious as to whether I won your little game.

What is the matter? Why so quiet? Surely something has given you pause.

But it was merely a figure of speech. There is no shadow. It was only a metaphor.

Now catch your breath. Calm down. I have no knowledge of what is to come.

I am not clairvoyant. I have no crystal ball. I was merely playing along with your guessing game.

I say the shadow is not a shadow. I didn't mean to cause alarm. You've been struck a blow, my friend – deeply wounded, it would seem – by a metaphor.

He put the pillow-case of money on the counter.
Please lock this bag of my money in your safe.

The Members of Parliament, Provincial and Federal – the Mayor of this Fair City – the Superintendent of the Racetrack – the owners of the winning horses – no horses, of course, on the platform – winning jockeys off to the side. The resident band huffs and puffs an opening tune. The half-time festivities are commencing. The judging will soon commence, my friends – but first a series of speeches from all concerned.

If they did blaze side by side.

Hope you all had a chance to see it – encased in its box in the stable-yard – couldn't leave it exposed to the flies in the afternoon sun – too bad it wouldn't fit in under the grandstand – it's a magnificent piece of cheese – made right here in Southern Ontario – by our friends in Ingersoll – how could such a little community rise to such towering heights?

A night and a day – half a day – of utter agony. Agony for my son – for my second wife – for me. He died as the clock struck noon – a kind relief. The doctor had done all he could. The bloody bandages we changed upon the hour.

He each winter the forest trees

A person running on deformed limbs.
A man with his eye on the target.
The kind of person who deals in ideas.

Did quickly hew them down with ease,

Will he have to leave someone there, behind, in the nether-world?
Someone he loved and lost long ago?
Will he be blinded with tears as he reaches the light of day?

For he to work had a desire
And the skill did soon acquire,

Now if you'll all just move out to the stable-yard - that's where the Mammoth Cheese now sits - no, there will not be any races while the judging is taking place - the wickets are closed for the interim - cooperate, please, or perhaps I'll have to consider closing the bar - we want everyone here to come out to the stable-yard - no, I promise you that it won't take more than ten minutes - twenty at most - we'll be done, I am sure, in a jiffy - there's only one block of cheese - I assure you the races will re-commence again when the judging is done.

He onward cheerfully did go.

"Poetry means something different to everyone who contemplates its charms. To some, it is the commonplace idea or sentiment dressed up in eloquent words. To others, it is the thumping rhythm of an old ballad. To some it is the crashing waves of a soul-tearing cry of agony from a Hamlet or a King Lear. Poetry appeals to us on an individual basis. Some will find pleasure in McIntyre's verses and some will not."

Chapter 14
Hamilton 3

A rustling in the crowd. Ingersollians and those who did not retire to the bar. Finally, a hush settles over the stable-yard. The crowd parts as the judges move to the fore. A sea of expectant faces. Not a soul would dare to breathe at this solemn hour.

That every word doth almost tell my name.

Does Hamilton know how important this is? Does Hamilton know how vital this designation will be for our community? It will be the very life-blood, the very brain-fluid, the very grey-matter of the soul of our future existence! We call on Hamilton to send us to England on the crest of a wave!

I carry paper

One drink of light and one of dark.
A story without suspense.
A sailor who has swallowed a compass.

and a pencil

How long were you a widower?
Did you raise your son on your own?
Was there any other presence in your life?

wherever I go.

The notes of the organ on Sunday morning.
The burning of brush to clear a field.
A lecture at the Mechanics' Institute.

A thought is a flower by the side of a road. A thought is a diamond in the shaft of a mine. A thought is a pearl on the ocean floor. A thought is a penny dropped into a well. A thought is an idea flung, as a bird will fling itself, across the arc of the sky.

May I behold in thee what once I was.

I told you it wouldn't be so terrible. I told you the current would not run too fast. I told you everything would be all right in the end.

A rebel camp at Missolonghi. Fighting to free the Ancient Greeks. A mosquito took exception. A raging fever assaulted the brain.

"Pretty grim what happened to his son."
"I was there in the store that day."

I pour the letters from a box unto a page! The letters flit like bees! They dive like dolphins! They tumble like acrobats! I wait for the letters to settle on the page!

Too busy to feel anxiety - sound the depths - a life-line, offered or denied - deeply wounded - keep your distance - not in control - come back today to life - holding something precious - there must be something - a golden mean.

I lost my only son – in an accident – at the store. I mention that just to head off any questions that you might accidentally ask. I'd rather stay away from that particular fact.

He was the son of my first wife and I. Memories linger, of course, from when he was a boy. To bury a child, as they say, is the most regrettable act there could be in anyone's life.

I've had two wives. My son was the son of my first wife. Years apart died my wife and my son – on the very same day.

They would catch a glimpse of each other
while passing on the flight-path.

A cheer goes up from the Ingersollians! A cheer that almost takes the lid off the box of cheese! We have finally been acknowledged! – not one effort has been in vain! Hearty shouts and back-slappings and the dancing of jigs! Oh to be an Ingersollian on this fair day!

Did ye not hear it? – No, t'was but the wind!

The great cheese sits on the wagon! – in all her glory! – inside her box! All the splendour of a sphinx made out of food! The great cheese smacks her lips, inside the cheese-box, in anticipation, as well she might! Soon she will be a tasty morsel for a Queen!

Alas the storm grew menacing. Alas his boat was sunk. Alas his body washed up on the shore. A book of poems in his pocket.

A set of weights and a balance.
Watching the judging in the stable-yard.

I pour a second box of letters onto the page! More bees, more dolphins, more acrobats! They flit, they dive, they tumble all over the page! The letters are made of ink! I wait for the letters to settle down in place!

Accorded full respect - all the way here - when the judging is done - boulders in my seed-field - room was tightly locked - something that it is seeking - planning and execution - some kind of unresolved aftermath - has to mean something - for sure and for certain.

My first wife and I met when we were young – it was a romance out of a book. A young apprentice at furniture-making – a furniture-maker's daughter. A gradual awakening to the possibilities and the promises of life.

My second wife and I shared a glorious rebirth. Well a rebirth for me, but not for her. Not for her, as she – unlike me – had not died.

We are carried wherever life takes us. Whether we steer our frail craft or not. And that, my friend, is all I will say about that.

I'm pleased to know that
said the man in the moon.

The lighthouse-keeper had the keeping of the lighthouse. He polished the mirror and kept the oil-lamp burning bright. All the ships at sea relied on the lighthouse-keeper. They steered safely into the harbour by his light. They relied on him to reveal the rocks and the shoals.

The paths of glory lead but to the grave.

Meeting in the church choir like that. A rather melodious place to meet and exchange a few words. I was pleased when you allowed me to walk you home.

A room near the Spanish Steps in Rome.
A lantern swinging in the dark.
A person who is not writing his autobiography.

I think of you, sometimes, as a block of gigantic cheese.

All of these cheeses would tickle the palate
Of the gods in their Olympic palace
When they all sat down to eat
After performing, each day, a mighty feat

Where did you meet your second wife?
Was it love at first sight or love delayed?

Do you remember the day that you proposed?

Humans, at their best, come close to thinking like angels.

A gift to all the loyal people of her great Dominion.
No doubt it would warm her heart to do this for her minions.

Every great epic starts with a will and a single idea.

Walk through the doorway. Not through the door. This is a very fundamental distinction to make.

Birds singing in a tree.
A dance on the floor of a new-made barn.
A quadrille party at Port Stanley.

Oh Mr. Harris has a problem of mammoth size.
It will call on all his wiliness to improvise.

Mr. Harris at the front of the railway car – waving the certificate that he is holding in his hand. He is surrounded by the other factory-owners. Any one of them could buy and sell the whole town. Large cigars are passed around. Matches are lit but no backs are patted. Mr. Harris's face is gloomy – the manufacturers' faces are glum.
To see the world in a grain of sand.
The Ingersollians in celebration – roars of laughter from the crowd. A request is sent forward to Mr. Harris. If it isn't too much to ask, Mr. Harris, could everyone in Ingersoll be allowed to get to see?

A quiet room by the Spanish Steps. Seeking a respite for his lungs. Nursed by friends and fellow creatives. Passing the torch to other hands.

"The young boy was comin' along pretty good at the manufactory."
"He was going to take over from his dad some day."

I have boxes and boxes of letters! Should I pour more boxes of letters onto the page! Will they flit and dive and tumble? Will they settle down into place? Will they ever give me a sentence that I can read?

To pay for the damage - no comparison - a soul-tearing cry of agony - returns to empty streets - slides into place - snag and break the plow - the still-beating heart - the mirror being you - what is my role - a plan and a route.

I have formed a bond with many people in my life. I think of a bond as like a glue in a furniture-factory. In a factory – as in life – there are glues of different kinds.

I formed a bond with my father. I formed a bond with my mother as well. Each was a very special bond which has lasted for life.

Every glue has a purpose – every purpose has a glue. That is all I have to say about my lost son. And that is all I have to say about my two wives.

One day the man got angry
and bent the impish clock's two arms.

The lighthouse-keeper knew all the old sea-captains. He knew a captain from every seaport in the world. All the captains would drop in on the lighthouse-keeper. The captains would tell tales around the fire. A draught of grog as the keeper lit the stove.

The key turns and the door upon its hinges groans.

The old schoolmaster reciting Robbie Burns. Hands folded on the desk, feet flat on the floor. I close my eyes and I hear Robbie Burns himself.

Poems torn into tatters. Scattered o'er the attic floor. Eagerly tasting of the arsenic. Let the world be cruel no more.

Disappointment in Hamilton.
A somber train ride home.

When to the sessions of sweet silent thought
I summon up remembrance of things past,
I sigh the lack of many a thing I sought,
And with old woes new wail my dear time's waste:
Then can I drown an eye, unused to flow,
For precious friends hid in death's dateless night,
And weep afresh love's long since cancelled woe,
And moan the expense of many a vanished sight:
Then can I grieve at grievances foregone,
And heavily from woe to woe tell o'er
The sad account of fore-bemoaned moan,
Which I new pay as if not paid before.
But if the while I think on thee, dear friend,
All losses are restor'd and sorrows end.

The jar of arsenic - i don't confine myself - a response, in art - continually losing and finding - think of something else - applying the whip - an interesting consideration - an absent crowd - no light whatsoever - what of that - a new beginning.

I like a cup of tea in the morning. I perform my ablutions like everyone else. All of this while the kettle is on the boil.

A cup of tea out on the porch. Know what I say as I sip my tea? 'Who wouldn't want to live here?' I always say.

In Ingersoll – in Ontario – in Canada. Rain or sunshine – winter or summer – spring or fall – every morning I feel the same. This place has been good to me and I feel I am giving something back. We can only give what we have, do you know what I mean?

I heard of the recent breach of security.
An unfortunate incident to be sure.

The certificate is passed along the railway compartment. A perusal and it is passed over the head or over the shoulder to the one behind. I can see the red ribbon and the large print. 'First Place for the Largest Block of Cheese.' The certificate moves from hand to hand. Gradually the joviality sags and the laughter ceases. Puzzled looks when some of the passengers turn around. The certificate moves along the aisle at a funereal pace. Grim lips as the certificate is passed to me.

Hold infinity in the palm of your hand.

I hold it in my hand – the red ribbon – the large print: 'First Place for the Largest Block of Cheese.' My eyes slide down the certificate – they come to rest on the finer print: 'This Is to Certify That as Exhibited this Day in the City of Hamilton and in the Opinion of the Most Highly Qualified of Judges the Ingersoll Mammoth Cheese Is the Largest Block of Cheese in Hamilton and District.'

I wrote a poem – a poor poem. What a silly thing to do. My son dies and I write a silly poem. At the time it brought some relief. At times, I think that I should tear it up.

And soon potatoes, wheat and corn,

A statue almost buried in the sand.
A phenomenon enclosed in a travel-box.
A fishing boat with empty nets.

They did the rugged stumps adorn,

How many years have gone by since your misfortunes?
Have you recovered from life's early blows?
Or are there scars that you sense will never heal?

And Jane did help him with the hoe,

And well she did keep her row.

All the sea-captains sat in the lighthouse parlour and told stories. But the lighthouse-keeper never told any stories. He always felt that he had nothing to say. He had spent all his life tending the lighthouse. The lighthouse-keeper had never been to sea.

I fall upon the thorns of life! I bleed!

A candle beside my easy-chair. Aware of my elbow as I move my pen. If this poem catches on fire it will be a great loss.

Chapter 15
Ingersoll 6

The baker bakes the bread. The ferrier shoes the horses. The general store sells dry-goods. And my store sells fine furniture.

It was heavy, dark, profound.

Back to the routine. Back to the everyday. The holiday is over. Ingersoll's herself once again.

I can stop

A sharp scythe at break of day.
A boy looking at the water in a well.
A person with his arms around the whole world.

and write a poem

So how will your epic poem end?
Will there be a homecoming of sorts?
Will the hero manage to find his way back again?

almost anywhere.

Hills and dales and fertile farms.
A log road through a swamp.
Sunbeams gleaming on the Grand River.

So what have I learned in my thirty-nine years? What learned and what forgot? About the same as the bird who builds a nest in the spring. About the same as the squirrel who gathers nuts in the fall. Children know right and children know wrong. They'll cheat in a game or play by the rules. Those children know about as much as they'll ever know.

An old man who had charge of field.

Writing a poem is like dipping your finger into the ink-well on your desk.

The ink flows into your finger and into your blood-stream and travels to your head and to your brain. It mixes with the blood as it travels around. Then, when the mixing is thoroughly accomplished, the inky-blood – the bloody-ink – flows back to your finger and into the ink-well. And then, you dip your pen in your ink-blood and you write.

What the flagpole that had fallen in the midst of battle? What the walking-staff which was sticking in the mud? What the will that was ever and always oh so willing? What the circumstances that were turning out to be weak? One feeble hand on his pen and one on his heart.

The ancient poets ne'er did dream
That Canada was land of cream,
They ne'er imagined it could flow
In this cold land of ice and snow,
Where everything did solid freeze,
They ne'er hoped or looked for cheese.

"Sure enjoyed them races in Hamilton."
"They left the Mammoth Cheese out in the stable-yard."

Standing on the balcony – with her Majesty – holding up a wedge of the famous Mammoth Cheese. Her Majesty waving to the crowd and whispering – in an aside – that she can't wait to get back inside and have another slice of that delicious, delectable treat. Afterwards, in the palace drawing-room, I read my poem:

We have seen thee Queen of Cheese
Laying quietly at your ease
Gently fanned by evening breeze
Thy fair form no flies dare seize...

Her Majesty is even more ecstatic than when she tasted the Ingersoll cheese! It is art over commerce! – the taste of the poem has trumped the taste of the cheese!

Don't want to stumble - was planning to interview - hope to be welcomed - nipping at his toes - seeds from exotic locations - forest is dark - supposed to cure - a profound experience - competition without a prize - leak in the boat.

The progress of the epic?

Well, I can't actually write the epic, of course, until the great saga has taken place.

The epic will be the record of the adventure of the Mammoth Cheese – a response, in art, to a profound experience of a major aspect of life.

*Life was so busy
that they never exchanged a word.*

The hotel rents rooms to Ingersoll visitors. The bank takes money in and gives it out. The stable grooms the horses and gives them their feed. The restaurant serves the meals three times each day.

Of shattered reason's flickering rays.

Herself but not herself. Saratoga – Toronto – Hamilton. The journey out and the journey back – what was sought and what was accomplished – what was gained and what was not. What to do in the aftermath. What is Ingersoll going to do with the Mammoth Cheese?

What the flagpole that was falling in the midst of battle? What the walking-staff which was sticking in the mud? What the will that was ever and always oh so willing? What the circumstances that were turning out to be weak? One feeble hand on his pen and one on his heart.

*A few years since our Oxford farms
Were nearly robbed of all their charms,
O'er cropped the weary land grew poor
And nearly barren as a moor,
But now the owners live at ease
Rejoicing in their crop of cheese.*

The news from Hamilton.
Taking stock in Ingersoll.

Who is the current Poet Laureate? Can a Canadian be awarded that post? Is it 'The Poet Laureate of England'? – 'of the British Isles'? – 'of the Empire'? What if her Majesty should thrust it upon me? How could I possibly refuse? I have my form – my rhyming couplets – so I could write ream after ream after ream. I could rhyme on any topic – any topic that the Queen might command. She would be my greatest supporter – and I, in turn, would be hers. 'The Art of Majesty – the Majesty of Art': Queen Victoria as a statue made of words.

Your own qualifications - communicate among themselves - an unread poem - shattered reason's flickering rays - alone in the crow's nest - never heard a word - having some thoughts - celebrate your attributes - talk to other thoughts - a solid sidewalk.

Yes, the experience, as far as the launching goes, is indisputably underway. The cows have been milked, the cheese has been processed, the plan has

been made and the Mammoth Cheese is now exhibited gloriously on display.
Its immensity of presence can never be denied.

The man in the moon
was half in the light
and half in the dark.

Well, there's always a future. That's definitely for sure. I'm only thirty-nine
so there's lots more future left for sure. And my second wife is younger than
me. Perhaps another boy – or, who knows? – a little girl. Best left around the
bend, where they might or might not be.
And lovers met around the fire.
A flower cannot bloom without a root. A nation's life-blood will wither if its
history is not well watered by the bronze of storied rhyme:

When this country it was woody,
Its great champion, Mrs. Moody,
She showed she had both pluck and push,
In her work, roughing in the bush.

A group of monks going for a walk.
A judge who is reading from the wrong card.
The need to be one of the herd.

And since they justly treat the soil,
Are well rewarded for their toil,
The land enriched by goodly cows,
Yields plenty now to fill their mows,
Both wheat and barley, oats and peas
But still their greatest boast is cheese.

I think of the times we had as prizes at a county fair.

Of fate or hubris or nemesis
A gift of agony or bliss
Destroying Troy or founding Rome
and finding for Aeneas a new home.

Will he be washed up on the shore?
Will he be holding something precious in his arms?
Will there be some kind of unresolved aftermath?

Angels can communicate with only their minds.

The photo would be shown around the world.
To show that Her Majesty has become enthralled

A great epic of a great people doing great things.

Be wise when it's time to be foolish. Be foolish when it's time to be wise. Divide yourself in two when the roads divide.

A spring of long continuous rain.
Children skating on the ice.
A sawmill powered by water from a dam.

Puzzling out the structure of my epic poem.

If a block of cheese sets out on a voyage, and there must be something that it is seeking, and it cannot be seeking itself – the block of cheese – and the hero of the poem cannot be the block of cheese, and what the hero is seeking must be some other prize than the block of cheese, and what the hero is seeking must be an indication of validation from a wise and trusted source, would it not then follow that the indication of validation from a wise and trusted source in my epic poem would be something concrete – a tangible token – which would be as clear and unambiguous as was – in the ancient story – the Golden Fleece?

But, unfortunately, under the present circumstances, I just cannot see what it would be logical to consider that validation-token to be.

Or – in thinking it over – alternatively – in alia manu – it now occurs to me – might it be not a tangible token at all, but some sort of fuzzy message – some sort of puzzle-producing message such as we find in the ancient stories as well? Might it not be akin to the baffling, boggling, irritating, mind-shaking, mind-quaking, cryptic words of an Ancient Greek oracle? One that no one can tell what it means when first heard?

This might – or might not be – a fork in the road.

Perhaps I need to give the topic a lot more thought.

Oh Mr. Harris sits in his office all night long.
The voice of destiny sends an idea with the rosy-fingered dawn.

An emergency meeting is scheduled, by the manufacturers, at Mr. Harris's factory. I no longer have any idea what number 'Emergency Meeting' this would be. The press will be excluded once again. A decision will be made and will be announced to the populace. A decision in the best interests of all concerned.

We fear to say and yet we must.

What does the hero do in mythology? Well, the hero does the same as the shopkeeper. The hero checks the shelves. Place the sword above the mantel – hang the buckler on a hook. Pencil and paper are the weapons for taking stock.

What the flagpole that had fallen in the midst of battle? What the walking-staff which was sticking in the mud? What the will that was ever and always oh so willing? What the circumstances that were turning out to be weak? One feeble hand on his pen and one on his heart.

And you must careful fill your mows
With good provender for your cows,
And in the winter keep them warm,
Protect them safe all time from harm,
For cows do dearly love their ease,
Which doth insure best grade of cheese.

"Always with a book tucked under his arm."
"He's probably read every book in that library a couple of times."

Shakespeare wrote of kings and princes. I'd be delighted to do the same. What is a rhyme, I wonder, for 'Albert'? There must be dozens and dozens of words that end in that sound. 'Stalwart'? – 'halberd'! The room is tastefully appointed. Her Majesty's personal halberd graces the wall.

There appeared the ghost of Prince Albert
On the battlements, brandishing a halberd,
In his habit, as he was wont to live,
His visor up, his message for to give:
'A message for you, my former wife and current Majesty.
A message which, if poured in your ear, will avoid a negative tragedy.
I have come here, temporarily, from my permanent home in the afterlife
To help you to untangle the fateful threads that, if not shorn, will serve to baffle life.
You will make the right decision, it is plain,
If you choose this Canadian poet to poeticize your reign,
For it has come to me in a frightening vision
That he will rescue your name – Queen Victoria – from immortal oblivi-on!'

"I shall write the poems, Your Majesty, by which, in future times, the splendour of your reign will come to be known. They will burrow their way into British hearts. They will bore their way into British brains. The bees that buzz around every English rose – the pail that drains the sap from every tree." She pauses while she swallows and clears her throat. "A knighthood!" I hear her say, emphatically, as she reaches for another piece of cheese. "So soon?" I protest, in reply. "You have only heard one poem – though I can see that you are impressed. Should you not delay the knighthood until the rest of my poems are better known? You could have them printed by the royal printer in bindings of leather and gold. I could read them to you in the evenings of a couple of weeks. When you hear my advertisements, I guarantee that you will not be 'not-amused'."

A frightening tale - travel like lightning - the scythe is at its sharpest - memories that are painful - explains the wonders - come up with another way - we lose ourselves - what to do in the aftermath - deeper levels of thought - continued to shine.

And as for the winning of the prizes – the achievement of acclaim – why that is as inevitable as the sun – in the morning – in the sky.

The sun rises, it crests at noon, and remains where it is throughout the day.

The Mammoth Cheese has already been created – in all its splendour – in all its size – in all its immensity of bulk – and it will go on, like the sun, to be the light that is pasted forever in the sky.

Now neither the clock nor the man
can tell accurate time.

That fire was pretty ferocious. Took out a whole city block. Then the river came up when the ice backed up in the spring and flooded the town. Nothing to do but explore the wreckage and assess the damage and roll up the sleeves. Without these disasters I wouldn't be owning a brand-new furniture-emporium store.

And high their muses flight did wing.

I feel my Scottish heritage to the depths of my aorta. A few lines to read at a dinner at the Douglas Hotel:

Scotia's sons to-night we meet thee
With kindly feelings we do greet thee
In honour of the land of Heather
Around the board tonight we gather.

What the flagpole that was falling in the midst of battle? What the walking-staff which was sticking in the mud? What the will that was ever and always oh so willing? What the circumstances that were turning out to be weak? One feeble hand on his pen and one on his heart.

To us it is a glorious theme
To sing of milk and curds and cream,
Were it collected it could float
On its bosom, small steam boat,
Cows numerous as swarm of bees

Are milked in Oxford to make cheese.

An assessment of the journey.
Requesting an interview.

Poetic thoughts the mind doth fill,
When on broad plain to view a hill;
On barren heath how it doth cheer
To see in distance herd of deer.
And poetry breathes in each flower
Nourished by the gentle shower.
In song of birds upon the trees
And humming of busy bees.
'Tis solace for the ills of life,
A soothing of the jars and strife,
For poets feel it a duty
To sing of both worth and beauty.

They always manage - is able to see - to hear yourself - there is no black void - something that it is seeking - take him to the heights - opening their tomb - another emergency meeting - half in the dark - to test the ice - perched on the topmost shelf.

As for the progress of the epic poem, I have jotted down some couplets from time to time.

But I need the actual voyage – the adventure, the quest – as a frame on which to hang the rhyming couplets – an envelope in which to deliver this soul-searing thought-experience to future readers.

Without the world-encompassing experience of the great adventure – the braving of the waves and the great shipwrecks and the washing up of the hero on the shore – they would just be images of cows and milk and cheese.

But I still have faith in your enterprise.
I know that your bank is the safest place in town.

The pending fate of the Mammoth Cheese. Too busy to feel suspense – too busy to feel anxiety. Thousands of little things need tending at the store. A store does not run itself. The door doesn't open – the shades don't close – unless a human hand is taking part. Yesterday's takings – tomorrow's bills. Everything has to be held in balance. One cannot run a furniture store with one's head in the clouds.

Thanking us for opening their tomb.

If an item isn't an asset – it's a liability. If an item isn't a liability – it's an asset. Stocktaking is as simple a task as that.

Now we close this glorious theme,
This song of curds and rich cream,
Subject worthy of our muse.
I pray not your ears to abuse.

Lines on the death of my son, Alexander Murray McIntyre:

His mother from celestial bower,
In the self same day and hour
Of her death, or Heavenly birth,
Gazed again upon the earth –
And saw her gentle, loving boy,
Once source of fond maternal joy,
In anguish, on a couch of pain.
She knew that earthly hopes were vain,
And beckoned him to realms above,
To share, with her, the heavenly love.

So much pain and so little compensation. Should I tear this poem up or let it stand?

No organs then they had to play,

A person walking on the edge of a cliff.
A story of the bursting of a grape.
One set of footprints in the sand.

But she could work and sing all day;

Will he gain the prize for which he has risked his life?
The prize for which his whole society yearns?
Have you thought about how you'll have your poem end?

In spring he did live maples tap
To draw from them the luscious sap.

I probably give a false impression. I write poems about a lot more things than cheese. In a small town, you can end up being labelled. I write about lots of other topics, but I'll probably be known as 'The Cheese Poet' for the rest of my life.
Who will into this vortex dive.
"The fastest bullet is that which travels closest to the ground. The same can be said of verse. You will understand the poetry of James McIntyre long before

you master the intricacies of thought of a poet like John Donne or William Blake. Plain and simple – direct and clear. No hidden meanings to explore. No Easter-eggs buried in lofts of hay. No Christmas presents for which you must hunt throughout the year. No Gordian knot of speculation to entangle you in its web. James McIntyre knocks softly and all you need do is open the door."

Oh! It was a cruel deed.

Locking up the store at the end of a good-long-day. Just a habit that is born of routine. In this town there is no need to lock any door.

Chapter 16
Ingersoll 7

A meeting at Mr. Harris's factory. The latest of many Emergency Meetings. 'Emergency Meeting Ad Infinitum'? Probably not – perhaps the final emergency-meeting of them all. The manufacturers all stand on an empty cart. The Ingersollians gather around below. The cart with the Mammoth Cheese is nowhere in sight. Throats are cleared – words are spoken – an attempt to pick up the pieces and put them back on the shelf. Mr. Harris is the one who doesn't speak.

Full worthy of a better fate.

We thought it best for all concerned - seeing the reality of the situation - no significant award has been achieved - to cut the cheese into pieces - too expensive to ship as it is - to label each piece 'An Ingersoll Cheese'- to ship our brand across the ocean - to try to establish a market overseas - offer a chance for all to buy shares in the enterprise - this is what we feel is best for all concerned.

But I come

A man standing on a porch.
A poet who writes occasional verse.
A visitor who is being interviewed.

to the river

So – do you still want to write that epic?
Your lyric poems not enough?
Your everyday poems that you write about Ingersoll?

as often as I can.

A toboggan sliding down a hill.
A choir of singing children.

Games on the Twenty-fourth of May.

No interview at this time – no interview at this time. Mr. Harris is sequestered in his office. There is so much left to do. He is sequestered – alone – in his office. No man has ever burned more midnight oil.

She spied thirteen imps all dancing in chains.

When is the journey ever over? When is the quest at a final end? Always a series of questions to answer. Always new paths that beckon us on. From an armada – to a single ship – to a piece of wreckage slowly drifting towards the shore. A single sailor – clinging, exhausted – after a storm.

No more poems from the pen that can no more write.

"His second wife understands him."
"In a way that no one else does."

A bucket
of rich foamy cream.

To ignore the rumours - turn them into rhyme - might or might not be - always making something new - an effervescent irruption - to make his way - grow a third ear - press my case - voices told him - gates and portals and doors.

And now, if you don't mind, I have a question for you – although I realize that you are interviewing me.

Not an interview-in-reverse – just a simple question.

I am asking myself as I ask this question of you.

He fell asleep
on a wedge of cheese.

Plenty to do at the furniture store. I have neglected the daily chores. Off gadding to Saratoga and everywhere else. I rearrange the chairs in the showroom. I count the money in the till. I wash the window and glance up at the sign. I take a broom and sweep the sawdust from the floor.

The bells did ring round his sleigh.

One can live or one can write. I should put all these notebooks away. Put them in a cupboard and close the door. No more sit on the bench by the river. No more scribble with paper and pen. Leave the writing to the indolently idle. I should drown my pen and my notebook and plunge back into the river of life again.

His talent the fuel that fed his funeral pyre.

Early morning in Ingersoll.
Walking through the town.

A bucket
of fresh cool milk.

Gods who manipulate things - all are important points - try to communi-
cate - something that he is seeking - have that within - a non-event - we had
a sign - no personal questions - paid much attention - not checking the ropes.

Just suppose – just suppose – as some of your questions – so hard-hitting,
so unrelenting – just might have implied.

That the epic adventure does not take place.

That it turns out that conditions are not propitious for the undertaking of
such a magnificent mythical quest.

He dreamed that the cheese
had a set of wings.

All the town returns to normal. The kids go by on their way to school. Every Sunday the hymns are sung. Every Monday the washing is hung out on the
line. People walk across the bridge. Avoid the puddles as they cross the street.
Every morning the sidewalks are swept. Every evening, all the storekeepers
lower the blinds.

Bare ruined choirs where late the sweet birds sang.

Most of the talk is of honey. Making the honey for the hive. Only a few
talk about shares and establishing a market overseas. A concert down at the
schoolhouse. A visiting minister preaching in the church. Everything pretty-
well restored or replaced from the flood and the recent fire. Nice to buzz about
all this gossip, but my watch insists on the time. Better get home or else I'm
going to be late for lunch.

A hero setting forth on a great adventure.
A community undertaking a major enterprise.
A chronicler of the history of his time.

I think of the future as two people meeting at sunrise on a bridge.

Whether tragedy or comedy
Always up to deviltry
With other gods in rivalry
They all enjoyed a meal of cheese
Left on the altar them to appease.

What size town did Dante live in?
Did Milton or Chaucer live in big towns?
Wasn't Homer just a shepherd who tended his flock?

Angel-children leave angel-imprints in the cloudy snow.

By the recipe for cheese that her subjects have created,
Whose success would no longer have to be debated.
The lady who is known as 'The Empress of India', if you please,
Would add to her nomens the 'The Empress of Ingersoll Cheese'!

The Iliad, The Odyssey, Paradise Lost and *The Mammoth Cheese.*

Looking up, all he saw was earth. Looking down all he saw was sky. He decided that it would be best just to stay right there.

A machine pulling up stumps.
A man sitting and writing a poem.
A store with an abundance of furniture.

Oh Mr. Harris's idea is a mammoth compromise.
It is to reduce the Mammoth Cheese to a manageable size.

Mr. Harris is not available. He is sequestered – alone – in his office. Cutting, packaging, labelling, corresponding. Cost of shipment – percentage of sales. Pick the pieces up and try to make them whole. Mr. Harris is immersed in waves of calculations. His head is bobbing amidst a paper-and-pencil sea.
He heard a gun – he was elf shot.
The hero washes up on shore. Picks himself up and wipes his brow. Finds a stream and drinks fresh water. Builds a fire to keep himself warm. Attempts to figure out where he has landed. Get a sense of the lay of the land. Things are strange and things are familiar. He knows not where he is. The casting ashore and the taking of stock. Is this a new and alien landscape or is it my home?

Only twenty-five years old and no more poems.

"I'll tell you he's written an awful lot of poems."
"Some day he'll have enough books to fill a shelf."

A bucket
of clear spring water.

A request for an assessment - sifting through the ruins - the trepanning of your head - reading from the wrong card - what is a light - not in vain - deeper than our thoughts - something that it is seeking - life's epic ecstasies - the laying of a cornerstone.

That the bold and wily hero does not undertake a dangerous voyage in treacherous seas.
That he does not wash up exhausted on a mysterious shore.
That he does not persevere and win the prize.

*The cheese lifted the man
and flew towards the sun.*

Carrying on at the furniture store. Discussing the faults of the new design. An easy-chair that causes the back to be sore. The old fellow who comes to sleep has found a flaw. What can we do to relieve the pain? An easy-chair should make life better, not make it worse.
In years that bring the philosophic mind.
Whether to abandon the mammoth epic? An epic task just to decide. I have lost the climactic ending. There won't be a London, a Paris, a Rome. The story begins and ends in Ingersoll. How can I make an epic of that? The Mammoth Cheese is being reduced to single-bite size.

A suffering seventeen-year-old King Lear.

Arriving at the furniture emporium.
Another day at the store.

*A bucket
with nothing inside.*

Heard the commotion - in the early morning - as inevitable as the sun - yield will be heavy - seal the door - meant to be - seem to go together - drifting on a river - any connection to life - have enough cares - ten-year contretemps.

That the story is not found to be suitable for the form of the epic.
That the things that didn't happen are the adventure – the regretted-alternative-adventure, as one might say.
How could such information – such unconsidered-information – such unvalued-information – such unpromising-information's – such destined-for-the-scrap-heap information – find, for itself, a literary form?

*The cheese melted
and left him stranded in the sky.*

A note is sent to my house. A knock on my door at the crack of dawn. It is the night-watchman from the cheese factory. I stand in my pajamas, on the porch. Meet me – says the note – at the factory. A message from the admiral of the fleet. An interview – at last – with Mr. Harris. An assessment of the quest for the Golden Fleece.

So brilliant in their glorious might.

The words I am feeling now must be rendered into print! – into ink that must never fade away! I have Ingersoll-blood in my veins! – we all have Ingersoll-blood in our veins! – we need no Saratoga-approval, nor Toronto-recognition, nor Hamilton-acclamation for validation of our worth! This I declare on behalf of the citizens of Ingersoll: the Ingersoll Cheese is bigger than the size of the British Empire! – it is the cheese that we have made right here in this town! The Mammoth Cheese is the biggest cheese in the whole wide world! My only thought for what seems like years has been the Mammoth Cheese! A smaller package – a different label – but the dream remains the same! I have curds and whey in my bloodstream! A piece of my heart will go to England with every slice of cheese! Every slice of cheese is a slice of Ingersoll!

It's hard to know what to do. When a son dies, do you write a poem or not? What are words? – where do they come from? – what do they do? My first wife was his mother. When my first wife died I didn't write a word.

He gathered it in big log trough,

An open door on a busy street.
The daily, weekly, seasonal routines.
The sun in winter, summer, spring and fall.

Then boiled it down and sugared off,

Why did they make up all those stories?
Why did they take the time to write?
What was the point of writing those epics so long ago?

Enough the household for to cheer,
With all its sweets for the whole year.

Sitting on my porch. It is evening. Time has passed. All the dust has settled down. Polishing a poem. My wife – beside me – sits and sips her tea. What a wonderful life I am living – every minute of every day is a wonderful life – every day is a wonderful life of many years.

The deep truth is imageless.

I think the thing that I have thought so often. In the morning and in the evening – as the sun climbs the ladder of the heavens – as the sun dips down behind the trees. Who in the world would not want to live here? Who would not want to live in Ingersoll?

Three Books

James McIntyre: The Mammoth Cheese– a novel
With the contribution of eight hundred cows, the tiny village of Ingersoll, Ontario, Canada has not only produced the world's largest block of cheese, it has also nurtured the epic poet who can rapturously sing its praises. Now, if only Queen Victoria can be persuaded to take a hearty bite and add her majestic voice to the poet's ecstatic hymns of praise, the Mammoth Cheese will become the edible jewel in the crown of the globe-girdling British Empire.

The Making of James McIntyre: The Mammoth Cheese – a reflective journal
This journal records the author's reflections on the process of the crafting of the novel as it evolved through the stages of planning, writing, editing and polishing. It constitutes an effort to be as conscious as possible of the process whereby the single idea that suggested the topic of the novel was expanded into a complex work of art. Topics range from the nuts and bolts of novel-building to the nature of the novel as an art-form.

Planning James McIntyre: The Mammoth Cheese – a planning notebook
During the writing of the novel, the author kept a notebook which records the day-by-day development of the novel as it found its shape and style. The notebook reveals how a vast cluster of thoughts was sifted, selected, structured and polished into novel-form.

The Project
Together, this novel, journal and notebook comprise the twenty-eighth installment in an on-going novel-writing project in which the author is exploring the concept of form and meaning in the novel, and of the novel as a form of expression in the 21st Century. All of the published journals and notebooks are available for free access at www.johnpassfield.ca.

About the Author

John Passfield was born in St. Thomas, Ontario, Canada, and continues to reside in Southern Ontario, near Cayuga, with his family. He is interested in exploring the development of the novel as an art-form, and has written many novels, planning notebooks and journals in his search for a form for the poetic novel of our time. He has posted many short readings from his novels on You-Tube, each with a note on novel-writing as a craft.

Novels by John Passfield

Grave Song
The Agony of Robert Chisholm

Jumbo
P. T. Barnum's Greatest Creation

Pinafore Park
The Swan Boat Incident

Water Lane
The Pilgrimage of Christopher Marlowe

Rain of Fire
The Ordeal of Conductor Spettigue

Victoria Day
The Fabric of the Community

The Wright Brothers
Flight is Possible

Leni Riefenstahl
The Valley of the Shadow

Out of the Park
The Cogitations of Babe Ruth

Raskolnikov
Murder with an Axe

Death Day
The Apology of Sergei Eisenstein

Einstein
Wonder

Geoffrey Chaucer
Canterbury Bound

Ospringe
A Visit with Grandad

Pompeii
Vesuvius Dominus

Beethoven
The Ninth Immersion
Job
The Cornerstone of the Universe

Bethune
The Only Person Alive in the World

Terry Fox
Somewhere the Hurting Must Stop

Lord and Lady Macbeth
Full of Scorpions is My Mind

Cyril Passfield
Out West

Glenn Gould
Light and Dark

Emily Brontë
More Myself Than I

L. M. Montgomery
I Gave You Life

Pauline Johnson
Know Who I Am

John Passfield
Saturday Morning

Eleonora Duse
Let Me Have My Wings

James McIntyre
The Mammoth Cheese

Shakespeare and Cleopatra
My Life Is Not My Own

John and Santa
The Cowboy Shirt

John and Cassandra
Fair is Fair

John and Dickens
A Christmas Mystery

See www.johnpassfield.ca for publishing information.

In Search of Form and Meaning:
Journals by John Passfield

Each journal is a day-by-day record of the complex process that a writer under-goes while crafting a work of art. It records the largest decisions, of structure and theme, and the smallest decisions, such as the choice of one word over another, and the constant interaction between the two. Each journal is a record of a writer's reflection on the craft of novel-writing.

The Making of Grave Song

The Making of Jumbo

The Making of Pinafore Park

The Making of Water Lane

The Making of Rain of Fire

The Making of Victoria Day

The Making of Flight is Possible

The Making of The Valley of the Shadow

The Making of Out of the Park

The Making of Murder with an Axe

The Making of Death Day

The Making of Wonder

The Making of Canterbury Bound

The Making of Ospringe

The Making of Vesuvius Dominus

The Making of The Ninth Immersion

The Making of The Cornerstone of the Universe

The Making of The Only Person Alive in the World

The Making of Somewhere the Hurting Must Stop

The Making of Full of Scorpions is My Mind

The Making of Out West

The Making of Glenn Gould: Light and Dark

The Making of Emily Brontë: More Myself Than I

The Making of L. M. Montgomery: I Gave You Life

The Making of Pauline Johnson: Know Who I Am

The Making of John Passfield: Saturday Morning

The Making of Eleonora Duse: Let Me Have My Wings

The Making of James McIntyre: The Mammoth Cheese

The Making of Shakespeare and Cleopatra: My Life Is Not My Own

The Making of John and Santa: The Cowboy Shirt

The Making of John and Cassandra: Fair Is Fair

The Making of John and Dickens: A Christmas Mystery

See www.johnpassfield.ca for free access.

The Novel as an Art-Form: Planning Notebooks by John Passfield

Each planning notebook is a printed version of the hand-written notebook which records the planning, writing, editing and polishing of each novel. Each notebook is an attempt to record, understand, and organize the vast cluster of thoughts which occur as one grapples with the various levels of organization which a clear yet complex work of art demands.

Planning Grave Song

Planning Jumbo

Planning Pinafore Park

Planning Water Lane

Planning Rain of Fire

Planning Victoria Day

Planning Flight is Possible

Planning The Valley of the Shadow

Planning Out of the Park

Planning Murder with an Axe

Planning Death Day

Planning Wonder

Planning Canterbury Bound

Planning Ospringe

Planning Vesuvius Dominus

Planning The Ninth Immersion

Planning The Cornerstone of the Universe

Planning The Only Person Alive in the World

Planning Somewhere the Hurting Must Stop

Planning Full of Scorpions is My Mind

Planning Out West

Planning Glenn Gould: Light and Dark

Planning Emily Brontë: More Myself Than I

Planning L. M. Montgomery: I Gave You Life

Planning Pauline Johnson: Know Who I Am

Planning John Passfield: Saturday Morning

Planning Eleonora Duse: Let Me Have My Wings

Planning James McIntyre: The Mammoth Cheese

Planning Shakespeare and Cleopatra: My Life Is Not My Own

Planning John and Santa: The Cowboy Shirt

Planning John and Cassandra: Fair Is Fair

Planning John and Dickens: A Christmas Mystery

See www.johnpassfield.ca for free access.

Other Books
by John Passfield

Oak Street
The Passfield Family

The Poetic Novel I
Influences and Elements

Intensities I
(1–100)
Verses on Various Topics

Intensities II
(101–200)

Intensities III
(201–300)

Intensities IV
(301–400)

Deepening Imagery I
(1–103)
Verses from the Novels

Deepening Imagery II
(104–200)

Deepening Imagery III
(201–214)

See www.johnpassfield.ca for free access.